Constellation

CONSTELLATION

☆

a novel ☆

☆

Greg Mulcahy

Avisson Press, Inc.
Greensboro

CONSTELLATION

Copyright © 1996 by Greg Mulcahy. All rights reserved. No part of this book may be reproduced, in any form, without permission from the publisher, unless by a reviewer who wishes to quote brief passages. For information, contact Avisson Press Inc., P.O. Box 38816, Greensboro, North Carolina 27438 USA.

First Edition
Manufactured in the United States of America

Library of Congress Cataloging-in-Publication Data

Mulcahy, Greg.
Constellation: a novel/Greg Mulcahy. -- 1st ed.
p. cm.
A portion of this book was first published as the short story "Franchise" in the author's Out of Work.
ISBN 1-888105-13-5
I. Title.
PS3563.U389C66 1996
813'.54--dc20
96-2755
CIP
A portion of this book first appeared as "Franchise"; from *Out of Work* by Greg Mulcahy. Copyright © 1993 by Greg Mulcahy. Reprinted by permission of Alfred A. Knopf Inc.

For Pete, who might have thought it funny.
— G.M.

Wayne drifted for awhile. He bummed around Europe. Held odd jobs, got married. When the marriage and everything else fell apart, he was desperate. He could not believe he would not go crazy, or be murdered, or get cancer. Wayne hooked up with a group. He would wake up shaking at night and pray and pray he would not get cancer. Those years were the hardest thing to believe. Incredible, the things he did. He moved away from the group, got a bookstore job that lasted. By the time he made it home, his father had been killed in an industrial accident and his mother had remarried. The new stepfather did not care for Wayne. Wayne did not care for the stepfather either. His mother and the stepfather moved to Florida.

Wayne had an apartment but he did not have a job and he needed money so he went to see his brother.

Bob was a doctor.

—Are you okay? Bob said.

—Nothing wrong with me, Wayne said.

Bob looked haggard. Perhaps he was putting in long hours in the Emergency Room.

—And you? Wayne said. Feeling fit?

Bob leaned back in his doctor's chair, opened a drawer in his doctor's desk, took out a bottle of tablets. He shook a few into his hand, swallowed them. —Want some?

Wayne held out his hand. —What are these?

Bob shrugged. —Vitamin supplement.

Wayne swallowed the pills. —I'm here about money.

Bob laughed.

—Don't I have some coming?

—Yes. Bob laughed harder. —In theory, you do. What Mother didn't get, you and I share. The question is, what didn't Mother get?

—What?

—She took the cash and portfolio. The partners, lawyers, and tax people cut up the business. Liquidated it; I believe that's the term.

—Nothing? Wayne said.

—Dad always said to diversify. Remember the bar and the fast food joint? I got the bar. Had the bar. Shortly after I obtained it, it burned to the ground. Flaw in the wiring, I'm told.

Wayne smiled. —But I have the franchise? And some profits in escrow?

—Not the profits. Lawyers got those. And the franchise isn't a franchise.

—Whatever the technical term is, Wayne said.

Bob picked his fingernails with a letter opener. The opener looked like a black plastic knife. The name of a drug company embossed on it in gold letters.

—You're quite correct, Bob said. It was a franchise. But Dad cut some corners toward the end and the head office ended his affiliation. After that, naturally, business fell off. It's cut throat, that fast food.

CONSTELLATION

Bob lifted the tarp, rolled it back, gathered it into an awkward bundle.
—Amazing, Wayne said.
A yellow 1962 Mercury Comet with black interior, crumpled rear passenger-side fender, and long streaks of rust.
—Does it run? Wayne said.
—Dad meant to have it, Bob motioned to the tarp-covered mounds around them—these, restored. Somebody told him it was a good investment.
—But does it run? Is this the best of em?

The big signs were gone; their steel skeletons rose over the lot. The building looked pretty good. Brick and plastic. Windows covered with plywood. Across the street, a boarded-up car lot and burnt-out apartment complex.
Wayne walked to the back of the building. The lot was busted up; maybe his father got a deal on some defective asphalt. Weeds grew through the cracked surface. The drive-thru speaker had been ripped from its plastic frame. Rotting wire dangled in the wind. At the edge of the lot, brush and a wooded slope. All this would be woods. Failed development.
Wayne followed a faint trail. Cans, bottles and rags littered the hillside. A mound of trash bags with a halo of flies. He could hear running water in the gorge.
The banks were narrow ribbons of rock and sand. Broad stream, maybe thirty feet across. Wayne could not tell how deep it was. A log or a part of a car frame stuck out of the water downstream. Wayne walked towards it.

He heard someone humming. Singing. Half-humming and half-singing. Something hit the water. Wayne stepped back into the brush. The singing stopped.

A slight man with wild gray hair and beard, torn baseball cap, stained work clothes. The man held a long cane pole.

—Hey, Wayne called, getting any?

The man half-turned.

Wayne noticed the six-inch fillet knife hanging from the man's belt. He stayed put.

—Why? The man said.

—Just curious.

The man set the pole down, put one foot on it, and bent over a rock. He pulled up a piece of dirty clothesline, a crude stringer, hung with fat gray carp.

—Want to buy?

—Don't think so, Wayne said.

—No money? Take it out in trade. What you got to drink?

—How'd you get so many?

—Bait. It's all bait presentation.

The liquor store was small. Wayne looked for cutrates, local gin and vodka, bourbon with *Kentucky* on the label and *Wisconsin* in the fine print. Three liters and he came out less than twenty-five bucks light.

Wayne left the bourbon and gin in the car and carried the vodka to the water. The man was still

fishing. Wayne cracked the seal and handed the man the bottle. —What's your name?
 The man tapped the torn visor of his cap. —Bill, like on a hat. He pulled up the stringer. —Take your pick.
 —That's okay, Wayne said. We'll have a few drinks.
 They were three-quarters through the bottle, and it was getting dark. A breeze came up off the water.
 Wayne shivered. —Where do you stay?
 —That's where I come out ahead. Bill drank deeply. —I got my pick.

 Laughing, they went up the trail. Bill said, —We need a go-round tank. Water goes round and round. Put your fish in there, water runs through them, cleans them. Gets all the mud and that out. Then you know what?
 Wayne laughed, slipped on some mud, grabbed a bush. —I know what.
 —What?
 —I don't know.
 —Then they ain't gray-looking. Gold. They look gold. And sweet. Man, you don't know how sweet that flesh is.
 —It's the water, Wayne said.

 Wayne looked at the plywood covered window. —We need a hammer. Fucking sledge. Bust it to hell and gone and we're inside.

—C'mon, Bill said. You're drunk. He led Wayne to the back of the building and jumped up on a rusted out dumpster. —Follow me. He hoisted himself onto the roof.

Wayne followed. He had to jump twice to catch the roof.

Bill had a trap door open. —Careful, it's dark. He pulled a loop of rope out of the trap. —Catch the line and slide down. Wait till I'm down to start. Don't let go till you hit bottom.

Wayne waited for the call, slid down the rope. Bill lit a candle. A couple more. He sat down on an inverted pickle bucket and motioned Wayne to another. They were in the kitchen. The grills and counters were gone. Capped pipe where the sanitary sinks had been.

Bill spread newspaper on the floor, took out his knife, cleaned the fish. Wayne drank, lit a cigarette.

He finished the bottle. —We got more booze in the car. Should have got some food too. I'll go when I finish my smoke.

—Give me the keys; I'll go.

Wayne did not want to climb back out. He handed over the keys. Bill went up the rope. The trap door banged open. Everything was quiet for a long time. Wayne wondered if Bill had taken the Comet.

Bill slid down the rope, the bottles jammed in his armpits. —Why didn't you tell me?
—What?
—Which you wanted.
—Who cares? The Chinese call it all wine.

CONSTELLATION

Wayne opened the gin.

Bill rooted around in the dark, lit a can of Sterno, rigged a skillet over the flame with a homemade wire rack.

—Bread, they say in England.

—What?

—Call food bread there. Bill tossed a fish into the skillet. —Doesn't matter what kind.

Wayne handed him the bottle. —No, you're wrong. What you're thinking, you're thinking is, they call everything corn. That's what you're thinking of.

Bill handed Wayne the bottle.

—Any grain, Wayne said. Like oats. They call oats corn. And the funny thing is they don't even have corn over there.

—That ain't true. Bill flipped the fish like flapjacks. —What you mean is meat.

—Fuck you, Wayne said. Meat has nothing to do with it. Back then poor people didn't even eat meat.

—Back when?

—When they called it corn. You know, when they started calling it corn.

—That's when they called it meat, Bill said. Like, you know, the giant. The giant said, I'll drink his blood to make my meat.

—Giant? Wayne said. I never heard of any fucking giant.

Bill talked about the circular tank. Wayne concentrated on the fish and the bottle. He tossed the bones in the skillet and wiped his hands on his pants.

Bill looked at the bones, stopped chewing,

11

looked at Wayne.
—I own this place, Wayne said.
—No shit.
—Really. My old man had it. He's dead. Now it's mine.
—You can have the car dealer's across the way, Bill said.
—I'm not taking anything away from you. It's really mine.
—Anything is possible.
Wayne shrugged. —Who knows?
—Maybe I could work for you.
—Get this place going, Wayne said. A restaurant.
—Food, Bill said, on belts. Belt turns and the sandwich goes by. Man puts the catsup on. Again and again. All day long. Sometimes it seems like forever; that food never gives out.
—You'd be condiment king?
—Better than that.
—What can you do?
Bill stared evenly at Wayne. —I can find water with a stick.

They finished the whiskey and cigarettes. Bill wanted to take the skillet to the stream and scour it with sand. Wayne followed him out.
The sky was getting light. Wayne tripped on the broken asphalt and fell.
—Fuck, he said.
Bill helped him up. —Spring under here. Makes the ground shift.
—Sinkhole, Wayne said.

CONSTELLATION

Bill looked at Wayne, then at the lot. He dropped the skillet, went limp, bent at the knees, straightened up, stiffened stiff as a pointing bird dog.
—What? Wayne said.
Bill breathed hard. His eyes rolled back in his head. He breathed harder and harder.
Water burst through the lot like a hundred small geysers. Like little oil wells. Wayne and Bill were soaked. The water was foul; it smelled like rancid grease. It kept gushing.
—What? Wayne said. What?

—I didn't get interested in cars, Bob said, until I was over thirty years old. Other kids loved cars. Hell, when we were teenagers, everybody was nuts for them, and I simply did not give a damn. Now you know what I do?
Wayne had just got out of the shower. He stood there in his brother's robe towelling his head with his brother's towel. —No, Bob, he said. What do you do?
—I walk down the street and I look at them. Not just the ones I covet, all makes and models.
Wayne nodded.
—I cannot explain it to myself, this sudden interest, now.
—It's a mystery to me, Wayne said. Anyway, thanks for letting me use your shower.
—That's another thing, Bob said, I don't mind a bit. Why two years ago, I'd have been apoplectic.
—Maybe people change, Wayne said.
Bob opened a drawer in the vanity, took out a bottle of pills, shook a few into his hand, and popped

them into his mouth. —Sometimes a person gets disgusted. I get disgusted with myself, sometimes—the sloth, cowardice, meanness, greed, pride, envy, lust—if I let it, it can really wear on me.

He swallowed some more pills. —Thank God for these babies.

—You have a little gal someplace? Wayne said.

—Four or five scattered around. But don't mention them to Colleen.

The '62 Comet Bob had given Wayne died. Wayne had it stashed in a vacant lot, and he slept there, but it was only a matter of time until somebody found it and stripped it and burned it. Wayne had to think about what he was going to do.

Bob had said as much. Bob had implied that if Wayne would do something, anything, get a job of some kind, for example, Bob would help Wayne out. Wayne had to take the first step. He looked through the want ads.

Wayne found the application form confusing. He had to count backwards on his fingers to figure out when he had attended college and worked his last three jobs. There were questions about felony convictions and typing words per minute and foreign language fluency, questions that had no relationship to the job. At the end, Wayne had to sign a statement swearing he had not lied on the form.

The interviewer was a thick man with a bad

complexion. —You don't have a very steady work history.

—Well, I studied for awhile, you know, in and out of school. And then there's this economy.

—You don't have to tell me, the interviewer said. You'd be surprised who comes in here—lawyers, teachers, stockbrokers—we get all kinds.

The interviewer noticed Wayne had not put a phone number on the application.

—I just got back to town and I haven't had time to get one connected.

The interviewer told Wayne to call in a few days.

The woman on the line said all the jobs were taken.

Wayne showered at Bob's and told the story. —Maybe I was naive, but I thought the interview went pretty well.

—You didn't apply anywhere else? Bob said.

—I thought I had it sewn up.

Bob went stiff and white. His thin lips were taut over his teeth. —So what now? I work, Colleen works, Wolf is at school. I see what you're after, the run of the house. And you'll have it this morning, eh? Lounge about in a robe and watch my big screen while we contribute to society.

—I just want the paper, Wayne said, so I can look at the ads. I'm willing to chop wood, haul ice, shovel coal.

Bob popped some pills.

By the end of the day, Wayne had filed seven applications. He could not believe he had been such a fool; obviously the phone was the problem. He listed Bob's number as his own; surely his brother would understand the necessity of this move and make the answering machine available.

Wayne sauntered up the walk, admiring the shrubbery and home protection warning signs, stepped up on the neo-colonial porch, banged the monogrammed door knocker.

Bob's son, Wolf, opened the door. A sturdily-built lad, big for his age, with a hard-angled face. Wayne nodded approvingly.

—Is the old man home?

Wolf jerked his thumb towards the marble circular staircase. —Up there.

Wayne wound his way up the stairs.

—Who the hell is it? Bob shouted.

Wayne looked up.

Bob leaned over the railing, pounded his hands on its flat surface. —Who, goddamnit, who is in my house?

—The number, okay. Machine, okay. Bob knotted his tie. —Seven today, good, but it may take more, you know, it may take seven times seventy.

—Whatever, Wayne said.

—Let's take a little ride.

Bob talked while he drove. —You see these cases and you cannot do a thing. You do something. of course, don't get me wrong, but what does it mean?

—I don't know, Wayne said.

CONSTELLATION

—There is a thing, Bob said, called the old squeeze play. The I.R.S. on one side and the lawyers on the other, then throw in the administration and the patients. See, it's not just two sides anymore. Now they're all over the board.

—I understand, Wayne said.

—Do you have any idea how hard I've worked for what I've got? How hard I work to keep it, to just hang on? Bob pulled up in front of a sporting goods store. —This is it.

There were cases and cases and racks and racks of guns. Bob shook hands with the man behind the cash register. Wayne looked at a twelve-gauge shotgun with a huge rotary magazine. It was amazing. He fingered the price tag.

The man at the register boxed up a long gun and a handgun. Bob handed him a credit card, said something, laughed. The man smiled, reached down, placed several boxes of ammunition on the counter.

Bob gathered up his purchases. —Ready to roll?

Wayne lingered by the shotgun, running his fingers over the oxide finish.

—Yeah.

Bob breathed deeply, leaned back on the leather seat, put one hand in his lap and rested the other on the wheel.

Wayne settled back.

—Are you hungry? Bob said.

—No.

—Cause if you want, we can stop someplace. Chicken, whatever you want.

—No, I'm fine.

Bob frowned, shook his head. —I feel better now.
       —Good.
       —Law suit, huh? Take my license. You know what they say?
       —No, Wayne said. I don't know what they say.
       —They claim I sewed the mouth shut. But it wasn't me. I had nothing to do with it.
       —I'm sure, Wayne said. I'm sure that you did.
       —Like I left him with a mouth stuffed with cash.
       —Uh, Wayne said.
       —I will defend myself, Bob said. I will defend myself to the utmost. In the courts, in the hospital, in my living room, if need be.
       Wayne was very tired. He leaned forward and rested his head on the padded dash.
       —This stress, Bob said. I see it in my patients, and it, my friend, is the fucking killer. The Big Fucking Killer.
       Wayne slumped back in his seat.
       —Stay in one of the spare rooms tonight, Bob said. Tomorrow, relax. Eat. Wait for your call.

       After breakfast, Wayne looked through Bob's den. Medical texts and financial planning volumes on the oak shelves. He spun the antique globe, wandered upstairs. Bob and Colleen's bedroom was done in French provincial; Wolf's had motorcycle and cyberpunk posters on the walls. The spares were neutral, Van Gogh prints in white wooden frames.
       He went down to the living room, hit the

CONSTELLATION

remote, lay on the couch. Not much on the big screen. Wayne flipped around until he caught a war show on the educational station. Phalanxes of tanks moved across a field. The sky was gray, the tanks were gray, the field was gray. Wayne waited for the firing to begin.

Somebody gave a voice-over. The whole thing was just a training exercise.

The scene shifted to headquarters. A foreign officer talked about being a professional soldier. He said something about the discipline—the drill, physical training, kitchen duty, spit and polish—about how the discipline was designed not to teach the soldier how to kill, but how to die. The point was to learn to die.

After the war show, Wayne watched videos. No one called.

Wayne could not fault Bob. Bob had been generous. Generous in spirit. Down on your luck, Bob said, happens to everyone. I've been there, Bob said. Bob certainly did not blame Wayne. He had tried to help Wayne. Target one place, Bob said. Be persistent. Sell yourself.

It took a lot of talking, but Wayne got on as a stock boy at the gun shop.

When Wayne moved his cardboard box of possessions to the guest room, no one objected. Wayne worked second shift and slept mornings. He never saw Wolf or Colleen.

After a long shift of restocking ammunition, Wayne went to the kitchen.

Bob sat at the table, a glass of whiskey in front

of him. —You still here?
　　　Wayne got a beer and sat down. —I thought you didn't mind.
　　　—Mind? You see my life. You admire my living and think I have no complaint.
　　　—It's not like that.
　　　—There's a colleague of mine, Bob said, worked with the harshest chemicals. Experimental therapy. Good living, you think. You should see him now. Pickled alive. You get all that death, and you soak it in. Little bits, but they add up.
　　　—I'm sure, Wayne said.
　　　—To nothing, Bob said.
　　　Wayne stood up, tossed the can in the recycling bin, waved.
　　　—Watch your tail, Bob said.
　　　—Good night.
　　　—I can kill with a word, Bob said. Say *cancer*.

　　　On his days off, Wayne went out. If he could not make it back to the house, he spent the night in the back of the Comet.
　　　Wayne opened the front door. All he wanted was a shower. Colleen stood in her flannel nightgown crying. Wolf was beside her.
　　　—Quiet, Wolf said. He offered his mother a glass. —Quiet, now.
　　　Collen looked at Wayne and shrieked.
　　　Wayne stepped back. —Do you want me to go?
　　　Colleen buried her face in Wayne's chest.
　　　Wolf waved Wayne towards the kitchen.
　— Eat. It's okay.

CONSTELLATION

Wayne hesitated.
Wolf patted his mother's back. —There, there. He looked at Wayne. —We'll talk later.

Wayne made a sandwich. He ate, drank a beer, then another.
Wolf came in. —You have everything you need? I apologize for the scene out there.
Wayne had a mouth full of beer. He raised his hands.
—No, Wolf said. Please do not interrupt.
Wayne swallowed and sat back.
—Although we hardly know each other, Wolf said, you are my father's brother.
—I can be out of here in five minutes.
—Exactly, but you don't have to leave.
Wayne got another beer.
—You're part of the family, Wolf said, and there are some things you have to understand.
—You don't have to tell me anything, Wayne said.
—This has been a difficult day for my mother and me. A very difficult day. But he had to go. Wolf sat down. —It is not easy to express what we have suffered, what my mother has suffered, to an outsider. There was no other way. Let me give you just one example: for some years now, on weekends, my father would dress in rags and wander the streets weeping and singing songs of his own composition. Remember, this was a respected physician with a family and reputation to maintain.
—At length, Wolf stood up. Tears ran down his cheeks. —At length, he choked out the words,

—we could no longer bear the shame.

Wayne's boss was a Russian immigrant named Denis. Wayne started out stocking, but now if someone was sick or late, he worked the register. All the clerks had to wear handguns, but Denis let them choose their own weapons and gave them the pieces at cost.
—We don't want no one to even think about robbing this place, Denis said.
Besides, the pistols gave the customers the impression the clerks were serious and knowledgeable—experts.
—Advertising and security combined into one thing, Denis said.
Wayne chose a long-barrelled, single action .44 magnum with a tooled leather holster.
Everybody called him Cowboy.
Denis showed him how to steer the scared first-timers, burglary victims and homeowners in decaying neighborhoods and the mugged and senior citizens, away from the cheap under-powered automatics to the quality product, the one-shot-stoppers that, with proper maintenance, would last a lifetime.
—Walk the walk, talk the talk, Denis said.

The money was not great, but Wayne stayed rent free at the house. Wolf and Colleen were happy to let him stay on. And Wayne made himself useful cleaning, fixing things, doing dishes.
Wayne was glad to have the job, and since he worked, he felt he was entitled to a few small comforts.

CONSTELLATION

He bought a boom box, a few cassettes, some boots. He did not buy all these things at the same time: each time Wayne was paid, he would pick out one thing he wanted and buy it. The rest of his money, what was not eaten up by expenses, he saved.

    Wayne went to the mall. He planned to buy a shirt, but he saw a window full of watches, beautiful steel and gold things with real hands and numerals and rotary date dials.

    He felt his left wrist; Wayne had not owned a watch in years. —How much?

    The man looked at Wayne's clothes. —We have some nice digitals. Lots of buttons.

—The stuff in the window.

The man named his price.

—For a watch? Wayne shook his head.

    Another store. Wayne found a revolving plastic column. The watches looked like the ones at the first store. Knock-offs. Wayne bought.

—When you get time, Wolf said, we need some new light bulbs in the garage.

—I'll get right on it.

    The bulbs, cleanlng supplies and paper products were stored by the case in a big room on the third floor. Wayne noticed a door at the far end of the room. Tried it.

    It took him a minute to find the light. No wall switch, he waved his arms in the dark until he caught the cord. Room full of radios. All shapes and sizes: giant tube models with lighted dials, portables, transistors, table sets—units reflecting the manufacturing advances of the last sixty years, but not

grouped in any evolutionary order. Two battered easy chairs. Maze of cords and power strips on the floor. Wayne mentioned the radios to Wolf.
—That junk. Another of his so-called hobbies.

Denis had a daughter. Maria. Maybe twenty-five, dark hair and eyes, slender. She wore high, slick looking boots and a fur jacket. Wayne could not tell if the jacket was real fur.
He asked her.
She slipped away. —Pappa.
Wayne got back to work.
—Don't talk to my daughter, Denis said. —Don't look at my daughter. Understand?
Wayne nodded.
—If you think about her, I will kill you.

—What does that store do a month?
—I don't know, Wayne said. A lot.
—I was thinking, Wolf said, has your boss ever talked about selling the place?
—Never, Denis said. Never. Never.

—Bad news, Wolf said.
—There are other stores, Wayne said. Besides, it's a lot of paper. Fucking government's always over your shoulder.
—That's not the news, Wolf said. Dad's dead.
—Bob? Wayne said. My only brother?

CONSTELLATION

—Found him in a car; he'd run a hose from the tailpipe.
—I thought he'd been dead, Wayne said. That's the funny thing. I figured he'd been dead for months now. Since he, you know, left.
—Naw, I had him stashed in a rest home, Wolf said. Guess they don't watch them too close; somehow he got out and got that car. Wolf inhaled deeply.
—Fucking Chrysler.
—Hell of a note, Wayne said.
—Can you blame him?
—I can't blame anybody for anything anymore.
—Good, Wolf said. Anyway, maybe you want to go out. Going to be a hell of a scene when Ma hears this.

Wayne knew he was not supposed to look. Wayne looked. He looked at Maria. He watched her reflection in the antitheft mirrors. He thought about that coat. That fur. Maybe he had just said the wrong thing.

Wolf had Bob laid out in a plain wooden coffin in the front room. Colleen had been drinking. She and Wolf sat in straight chairs at the foot of the bier, a portable bar off to the side. Wayne poured himself a whiskey and sat down.
—He rose by his own weight, Colleen said. Pulled himself after his own star by education.
—For Christ's sake, Wolf said.
Wayne drank, said nothing, got another drink.

—You, Colleen said. You're the cause of it.
—I didn't do anything, Wolf said.
—What about you, Wayne? Colleen said. You remind me of Bob, of the best part of him.
—Nothing, Mother, Wolf said.
—The night he left? Colleen said. Didn't you fight?
—Maybe I stuck something in his mouth, Wolf said.
—Some medicated gauze, Wolf said, to quiet him down.
—Okay, Wolf said, call it a rag. So I put a rag in his mouth.
A bottle of gin slipped from Colleen's hands and shattered on the floor.
—This is metaphorical, Wolf said. He looked at Wayne. —I'm speaking in metaphors now.
Wolf walked to the coffin and pulled open Bob's mouth. —Let him talk now.

Wayne snapped a picture of Maria. Not a very good picture. He could not use the flash, and he had to get her while she was not looking. A side view. Dark, her hair and fur coat bluish, shimmering on the slick surface.
Wayne took his picture to the room full of radios and tried to get foreign lands on the short waves. Mostly he got nothing. Static, broken line of Dutch or Arabic, more static.
He would tune a radio, look at the picture, oblivious, until the static became too much, intruded on his consciousness; then he would get up and tune another radio.

CONSTELLATION

Wayne got something, an outdated jingle, maybe fifty years old, perfectly clearly:

Everything's fine,
Everything's great,
Since I tried,
Some fruit of grape.

He settled back to look at the picture.
Wolf kicked open the door. —That fucking Denis.
—What? Wayne slipped the photograph into his shirt.
—I offered that shit half-again what the place is worth, and the fuck won't budge.
—So what? Wayne said.
—So I want it.
—What for?
—Who knows? Wolf said. I want it and now I have to have it. I'm asking myself how you can help me.
—I don't think I can help.
—Can't help? Look at the future. You want to be caught in the collapse? We have to shore up our position, shore it up by any means, while we still can.
Wayne looked at his nephew. —All this, and you're only seventeen.

Wayne got his pistol out of the holster, but he forgot to cock the hammer, so when he pulled the trigger, nothing happened. Somebody hit him with something. When he woke up, it was all over.

Wolf, drunk, was drinking vodka from the bottle. —The Ruskinov got shotinov deadinov. Wayne turned on a radio.

Drink it down,
Go to town,
Don't let no one
Come around.

—Is this all we ever get? Wayne said.
—Poor country. Got some money to play these ads. Long time ago. Now they're all they got to play.
Wolf snapped off the radio. —Let's get something to eat.
—Let's go get laid, Wolf said.
—Hey, Wolf said, let's go kill some poor people. He fell, laughing, to the floor.
—You better worry we can trust those guys, Wayne said.
—I know em from school. They're okay. Worry about the widow. Smash a few windows; leave some dead rats around. Use graffiti; you'd be surprised at the power of the word.
—I don't know.
—Don't worry, I'll give her something. She can take the kids to Israel.
—I don't think they're Jewish, Wayne said.
—Well, Ireland then. Wherever. Belguim.

Wolf moved a rocking chair, Colleen's chair,

CONSTELLATION

into the radio room. —She says she wants to hear some music.
—I'm ready to be with people again, Colleen said.
—She can have my place, Wayne said.
Colleen stood behind Wayne's chair and stroked his head. —Why don't you stay and talk? Sometime's it's like you're not a person.

Wolf fired the employees at the gun store and made Wayne manager. —Shouldn't be difficult. Hire quality people and the place will run itself.
—Yeah, Wayne said. I'll get the best.
—Things will only get worse, and when they do, we get richer, Wolf said. We've got a fucking cash cow.

Wolf called Wayne into the office—Wayne's office. Wayne was not sure whether to take the desk chair or the visitor's chair. He brushed past Wolf and sat at the desk. —What's the problem?
—Suppose you spent your time sitting in a room all day thinking that someone was going to bring you a wonderful present?
—Yeah?
Wolf cradled his head in his hands. —Something must be done.
—The receipts are fine, Wayne said. A little slow, but we'll clean up at Christmas.
—If you were to marry her, all our problems would be solved.

—We'd be a family again; that's what she's always saying, Wolf said.
—This would be good for you, Wayne. It would really cement our relationship, Wolf said.

Wayne saw the matted clumps of fur on the freeway after the wedding. —Dead.
It's slush, Colleen said.
Wolf was in the back seat.
Wayne pulled over to the shoulder and stopped. —I have to take a leak.
—Me too, Wolf said.
He jumped out of the car. —I know it wasn't your first choice. Sometimes you have to take your second choice.
—I see them, Wayne said. Never miss. All the dead animals.
They got back in the car.
—It's slush, Colleen said.
—I want to sleep, Wayne said.

Colleen bought all his clothes. This time it was a gray suit with a chalk stripe. Wayne hated it, but he knew, as he put it on, that it would look great. The suit and the tie—some regimental pattern, as though he were a Sandhurst graduate.
Wolf tapped on the door, stuck his head in.
—We're all set.
—Okay.
Wayne sat in the chair he was supposed to sit in. The camera man had a pony tail, and there was a

CONSTELLATION

woman in black with cue cards. Wolf and Colleen stood back, behind the lights and cables, watching. The camera man pointed to Wayne.
—Hi, Wayne read. —I'm Wayne Murphy, manager of TOTAL SECURITY.
—People look at me and say, Wayne, what do you use?
—Well, I've got the beautiful home, lovely wife, boat, cash. I've got the vanity plates on the luxury sedan. And to go with it, I've got the guns, the mace, the stun gun, flashlight, alarm system.
—Seems like the whole country is going up—murders, attacks, arson—families turning guns on each other. It's like, like cowboys and Indians.
—We're offering an opportunity to help people protect themselves, themselves and their families, a franchise.

—Hawaii, Alaska, what are they? Wolf said.
—They're it, Wayne said.
—Combined, population of what? North Dakota? Not even American. They got in, when, in the sixties?
—Fifties, Wayne said. Fuck the population. They're everything.
—Forget em.
—The only states we haven't franchised? How the hell do we advertise? TOTAL SECURITY in every state, that's a shot in the arm. We say we're in forty-eight, the lower forty-eight, that's piss up a rope.
—Wayne, be objective. Wolf lit a cigarette from the stub he was smoking. —Alaska we'll never crack. They all got guns, they protect themselves, they

31

won't get the urban fear thing. Hawaii, who knows? What language do they speak over there, anyway?
—They have a lot of Japanese. The Japanese love guns, just love them. They can't get guns in Japan. We, you and me, Wolf, could go to Hawaii, open a shop with a range, and make more money than we're making selling guns here. Wayne waved his hand as though he were displaying the room. —More renting guns than we pull out of here, the home office.
Wolf opened the miniature, Euro-style refrigerator, grabbed a half-gallon of malt liquor, cracked it, took a gulp. —Why won't you listen? He lit another cigarette. —You think if this shit mattered it wouldn't be taken care of? Trust me.
—I'm trying to get it taken care of.
—Relax. Wolf smiled. —Man, you ever get your blood pressure checked? We've sold 148 franchises. That's about what the market will take. Maybe we bust our asses and get ten, fifteen more, but at this point it's the law of diminishing returns.
—So we give up promotion? True, we are pretty well anchored.
—Yeah. Wolf took a long drink. —We could sit tight. But the government's cracking down, and every minute somebody imitates our chain. That's when you know you're dead.
—So?
—We sink or swim. Shame to let this go.
—We have a buyer?
—We borrow the corp into the ground, bury the money, leave the franchisees holding the bag.

Wayne took a long shower, towelled down, slipped into the Turkish cotton robe Colleen had

CONSTELLATION

given him, and went downstairs.
 Colleen was stirring up a pitcher of gimlets.
—Feel better?
—Yeah.
 She handed him a drink. —I think, sometimes, and this is not a criticism—
 —Uh huh. Wayne swallowed the drink.
 Colleen filled his glass. —You need to trust Wolf.
 —I know, Honey. Wayne sat down. —It's just, shit, I'm so outside here. It's like I'm the weird uncle or something.
 Colleen moved behind the chair, put her arms around him. —You know you're part of the family.

 Wolf had always taken care of them. The house, the car, the suit, the shoes Wayne wore—all the result of Wolf's uncanny acumen.
 Still Wayne had his doubts. Not about Wolf. Or Colleen. Wayne was secure. Comfortable. Rich. Why could he not enjoy his good fortune? His brother Bob had laid the foundation, Wolf had built upon it, Colleen had stood resolute in the course of loss and gain.
 And Wayne?

 Wolf had a new car. He had a new car every month when things were going well. During the two month slump when it looked like some hostile legislation would clear Congress, Wolf was stuck with a Mercedes convertible. A committee killed the bill,

and Wolf moved on to a Lincoln.
But this car was something different. A custom job or prototype like a futurized Packard with a giant airplane engine. Massive interior. Persian carpets for upholstery. The thing seemed a quarter-block long and a lane wide, but it handled like a dream.
Where Wolf got them, where they went, Wayne knew better than to ask.
Wayne looked at his subcompact and at Wolf's new car and at his subcompact again.
—It's his choice, Wayne said to Colleen. But ours does everything we need.
Colleen patted Wayne's shoulder.
The car started. Wolf lowered the tinted power window.
—Wayne, he said, get to the shop and take everything you want. Tomorrow, it's gone.
Wayne filled a cardboard box: pens and legal pads, mostly-empty rolodex, pictures of Colleen. The furniture was tagged, his guns were at home, his files shredded.
He went out to the lot.
Wolf's car idled beside Wayne's car.
Wayne waved, popped his hatch.
Wolf's window shot down. —Let's take a ride.

A two story cinderblock warehouse with three-door dock in a growing suburb.
—New headquarters, Wolf said.
Wayne frowned at the block wall. —Couldn't we get something better?
—Not at this price. Wolf removed a padlock and pulled up a dock door. —Look at this place.

CONSTELLATION

Wayne looked. Block. Cement floor. Huge.
—Pristine, Wolf said. A fucking shell. Only used once. You know what they had in here? Grapes. No shit. From South America or someplace. They'd take the grapes out of crates, put em in those little green things, wrap em, and out the door. Great, huh?
—I guess so.
—No wear and tear. Grape falls on the floor, so what?
—Yeah, great.
—This space we can subdivide, partition, run in what we need, run it out. Change overnight. Versatility.
—What are we gonna do?
—TV, Wolf said. I got a satellite operation for peanuts. All we have to do is develop the programming. We can lease the equipment for nothing.
—Start with a security show—I had to give the franchisees that, call it promotion for em. We bill the shift as a responsible move, wealth creation for our partners, and bust out later. Nobody can touch us. We're in communications.

Wayne raised the window sash six inches and picked up a drill. —This is a simple but amazingly effective way to secure wood-framed windows in the older dwelling.
He drilled through the sash and frame.
—I want to be sure to deeply penetrate both surfaces and get well into the outer frame.
Wayne put down the drill and picked up a four-inch machine screw. —A simple screw. Any

strong nail will work just as well. He pushed the screw through the holes. —Now we have plenty of air flow, Wayne pulled up on the sash, —but the window cannot be raised beyond this point.
    —Stop it, Wolf shouted. Cut, goddamnit.
    Wayne turned towards the director's chair, blinked at the lights. —I thought it was great.
    —You're fine, Wolf said. He turned to the teenaged boy and girl camera operators. —It's you two. One more experimental shot and you both get F's.
    —But Boss, the girl said.
    —I'm not putting this shit into the teleprompter for my health, Wolf said.

    Wayne stared at the editing monitor. —Maybe if we add an assault rifle review?
    —That won't save us, Wolf said. Three more shows, minimum, and the fucking franchisees are already threatening to sue.
    —We're stuck?
    —No. They get out, but not through the courts: Let em cancel us. Our end's contractual, and they're off our ass.
    —Make the last three worse? Wayne said.
    —Yeah. Wolf paced the cement floor. —Businesswise, yes. But I'd like to make one, just one show that wasn't shit.
    —Personal satisfaction?
    —Why not? But how to do it?
    —How about a raid? Wayne said. The two of us battling multiple attackers.
    —Against eight or ten? Maybe. Let's see, we

CONSTELLATION

don't want any controversial stereotypes—
—Ninjas.
—I don't know. Pure action, we lose a certain human element.

    Silent, half-bent, their black suits blending with the night, four ninjas crept across the lawn. Inside the house, Wayne sat on a recliner, his feet up on the extended hassock. He had a pipe clenched between his teeth, and he was leafing through a newspaper. A golden retriever lay on a circular throw rug beside the chair.
    A smoke grenade exploded through the picture window. The dog was up, barking. Out of nowhere, a sword-wielding ninja warrior decapitated the beast. Wayne had a pistol-gripped shotgun in one hand and his .44 in the other. He fired casually, from the hip, hitting one ninja after another in the smoke filled room. The dog killer lunged toward him. Wayne stumbled, pressed the .44 against the man's abdomen, fired. The ninja fell backwards.
    The director, a girl with her hair tied back in a bandana, was on the set, screaming, —You killed the fucking dog.
    Assistants cleared the smoke with powerful fans. Three of the ninjas stood in a corner, their hoods off, smoking and drinking mineral water. The fourth ninja lay on the set where he had fallen. An assistant gave him mouth-to-mouth.
    —He's okay, Wayne said. I have blanks.
    The kid turned from the fallen warrior.
—Wadding, asshole.

—The actor's fine, Wolf said. Ruptured spleen and maybe some trace brain damage, you know, oxygen deficiency, but the insurance settled the wife. Everything's fine.
The house set had been dismantled; they faced blank walls.
—Thanks, Wayne said.
—Don't worry about it, Wolf said. The only problem is the footage is useless. The cruelty prevention people could prosecute. I can't believe that fucker went nuts like that.
—Too involved in the role, Wayne said.
Wolf opened a bottle of whiskey. —I guess you showed him. That is, if he remembers anything.

Wolf got a lawyer to declare HOME SECURITY NETWORK THEATER bankrupt, bought out, and liquidated by its new owners, a holding company in the Caribbean. He had Wayne fill out certificates of appreciation for the high school interns, and he incorporated the new network as FAMILY SOLUTIONS. Wolf had planned to go to a twenty-four hour European soft porn format, but the lawyer warned him off the idea.
—So, Wayne said, where do we go with it?
—The adult concept is still alive, Wolf said. I just hadn't looked in the right direction.
—What the fuck does that mean?
—Every adult is miserable, right? So we go adult inspirational.
—No, Wayne said. God no, no religion.
—I mean all your problems are because you

were treated like shit when you were young.
—Oh, that.
—Fucking gold mine. Play the same shows over and over. These assholes study them.
—Where do we get the shows?
—Big treatment complex in Minnesota, Wolf said. Once we've got a solid audience of doubt-filled weaklings, the advertisers will be beating down the door.

Wayne took over as engineer and announcer, working the board in the darkened studio and reading weather reports and program notes in the dead time between taped programs.
Wolf took off. He said he needed time to himself to plan his new show. As long as they had the network, Wolf decided to produce a series, something a little different than their usual human development offerings.
Wayne sat in the booth, drinking coffee and smoking cigarettes, listening to the language of failure and despair, loneliness and guilt, shame and fear for hours on end.
Five weeks went by.
Wolf kicked open the booth door. He was wearing a stained white suit that looked too small for him and holding a leash in one hand and a half-empty cognac bottle in the other. There was a bruise on his forehead, he needed a shave, and he had gained fifteen or twenty pounds.
—Wayne, meet the newest member of our network family. Wolf yanked the leash and dragged an animal into the booth.

It took Wayne a second to recognize the animal was a dog. A low, fat dog, its belly hanging almost to the floor, its body covered on one side with dirty white fur, the other side a naked mass of pink scar tissue. Pronounced bluish-black tumors dotted the skin and fur. The face was pushed in, a dull glimmer in the bloodshot eyes, bit of tongue and strands of slobber hung from the half-open mouth.
—What happened to it? Wayne said.
—Accident. You know those damn butane lighters.
The dog's short legs were bent beneath its weight.
—Meet Sponge Boy, Wolf said.
—What breed is he?
—Not sure. I think if a daschund were a toy, he'd be full size.
—Toy?
Miniature. Anyway, he's a mix. Looks to have a bit of bear dog in him, don't you think?
—Listen, Wayne said. We need to hire an engineer.
—Kid's show, Wolf said. Bear Dog Theater. Can you picture it?

Wayne slept for twenty-nine hours, his slumber troubled by dreams of those terrible shows, the men with odd haircuts going on about adulthood and dependency.
Colleen brought him a tray: coffee, juice, ham and eggs. Flower in a vase. Newspaper, not the local, the big one, neatly folded.
—Feeling a little better? She opened the

CONSTELLATION

drapes and put a CD in the player. —Eat now. Take your time. I'll be downstairs.

Wayne ate, looked through the paper, lit a cigarette. Finished his coffee. Read a piece about an opera.

His bare feet on the clean sheets.
His life.
Now.

Wolf got a new engineer and ordered a bunch of t-shirts and baseball caps emblazoned MEDIA MOGUL.
—You've earned some time off, he told Wayne.
—Here, take a shirt and a cap.
Wayne sat in the bed, clutching the hat and shirt.
—Now that FAMILY SOLUTIONS has a core audience, we have to continually develop em, Wolf said. Tell em they eat wrong, drink too much, are bad for their kids. Let em know their houses are filled with radon and crime is going up and our enemies are rearming. We must make them afraid within and without.
Wolf and Sponge Boy moved into the studio for a period of intensive product development.

Wayne sat in the room full of radios:

Don't put me on that lonesome track,
To speed away and never come back.
My back is heavy, broke by the load,
Don't run me down that Milwaukee road.

—What if we cleared all this out?
Wayne almost jumped out of his chair.
Colleen.
—Huh? Wayne said.
—Junk this crap.
—You could. Do whatever you want.
—I said we, Colleen said. Why don't we do something?

—I heard something, Colleen said.
Hot night. Their bedroom windows open.
—Downstairs, she said. Maybe outside.
Wayne nodded. The long guns were locked in a safe, but he kept his .44 in the bedside table for emergencies.
Wayne crept down the stairs. He stopped on the landing off the house-long hallway.
Nobody.
Hall, dining room, kitchen, breakfast room, den—all empty.
Wayne pulled the drapes open and looked out the picture window. Security lights along the front walk like runway lights at a deserted airport.
He listened. Not even the nervous neighbor dog barking.
Wayne stepped out the front door, his bare feet cold on the plastic WELCOME mat. He slipped quickly around the side of the house, moved toward the garage.
The quick sound of movement; footsteps on the drive.

CONSTELLATION

A man running away.
Wayne raised the pistol.
Too late.

Wolf was home.
Wayne could hear him downstairs talking to Colleen. Hear their voices over the buzzing of the radios. He tried. But he could not make out the words.
He opened the door and sang loudly:

You took it all and left me gone,
You squandered entire the fortune I won,
I only want, Baby, what is mine,
Don't leave me to that old Soo Line.

—He's never been on a train in his life, Wolf said. Where does he get these fucking songs?
—All he does is sit in there, Colleen said, and talk to himself for hours.
—What the hell does he have to talk about? Wolf said.

Wayne lay in Colleen's arms. He nudged her.
—Hmmm, she said.
—You notice anything different?
—Better, Colleen said. She kissed his forehead. —Better every time, Honey.
—I mean these dots, Wayne said.
—Dots?
—I have these dots all over me. These tiny red dots.

Colleen sat up and switched on the lamp. —I don't see anything.
—They're tiny, Wayne said. Look close.
—I think it's a symptom, Wayne said. Vermin. Lice or maybe fleas. Two kinds of fleas, you know. Human and animal.
—Do you itch? She said. I still don't see anything.
—The human variety aren't too common in America. But we have them here.
—I check myself, Wayne said. I want to get one, you know, a specimen. Something to take to the lab.

A man was pressed against the french doors of the patio. Face, body jammed against the glass and wood. Wayne looked at the man.
The man was still.
Wayne tapped on the glass.
No reaction.
Wayne stepped back, stepped in, punched, his fist stopping a quarter-inch from the glass. Nothing.

Wolf dragged the stiff man into the house.
—He's dead? Wayne said. Dead, that'll teach him. Rid of the fucker.
—No, Wolf said. He gently laid the man out on the floor. —Just stiff.
Wayne bent over the man and pulled off the man's torn cap. —I know him. Get a blanket; we've got to warm him up.

Wayne ran in circles around chairs, rolled on the floor.
—What's wrong? Wolf said.
Wayne ran in place, bobbed and weaved. —Things keep flying at me. He flopped onto the floor and did sit-ups.
—You need help? Wolf said.
—They can give you a shot, I hear.
—You want a shot?
—They put that big needle right in there, Wayne said. He stood up. —Hurts like hell going in, but then you get your relief.

The county hospital released the man Wayne and Wolf had found on the patio. Wolf hired him as a gardener/caretaker and gave him the room over the garage.
—I think he's a little off, but harmless, Wolf said. And I think he's a friend of yours, eh Wayne?
—Not a friend exactly. More of a weight around my neck.
—If he's a problem, say so. We can get him taken care of.
—Not so easy to solve, Wayne said. Let him stay.
—Bill, Wolf said. He said his name's Bill.
Wayne smiled. —He did, did he? And your mother, what does she say?
—She doesn't say anything.
—So you've got it all planned?

—Planned? Wolf said. Where's there any fucking plan?

—You should see someone, Colleen said. Any doctor you like.
—For what? Wayne said. He stood in front of the full-length mirror in their bedroom. —Do I look bad? My weight's steady. Appetite good. I could drop ten pounds maybe, but that's just a matter of exercise. He pulled up his right eyelid. —No jaundice that I can see. More gray than yellow, in fact.
—Maybe just a check up, Colleen said.
Wayne had his forefingers on his left wrist. —Pumping strong and well within the normal range.
—Please, Colleen said. Do it for me.
—You're right; I'll start tomorrow.

The studio was fifteen miles from the house. Too far. But the park was only two miles. A perfect distance. Wayne would not run. Not at first. Maybe later. Plenty of time to work up to that.
For now, he walked.
Walked to the park, sat for a few minutes, walked home. Every morning. Walked around the park. There was a little brook with wooded banks. Wayne followed the banks, looking at the trees.

Bill was working in a flower bed in front of the house when Wayne got back.

CONSTELLATION

—There's your joke, Wayne said.
Bill leaned on his shovel.—And what's yours?
—You with a shovel. What are you digging up?
Bill pointed to the turned earth. —The bed.
—Don't go too deep.
—Just bust the clods, Bill said. That's step one.
—Then?
—Later I'll do my planting.

Wolf drove Wayne to the station in a red sportscar.
—You've got to see this live. After that, there's plenty of tape you'll want to review. In fact, I'm gonna sell the shows on cassette if I can't get some syndication.
—Be good to keep control, Wayne said.
—Whatever brings the quickest return. All things equal.
—The more control we have, Wayne said, the safer our position. Never lose control.
—Yup, Wolf said. He pulled a liter of gin from beneath the seat. —Open that for me, huh? Oh, and help yourself to a drink.
Wayne cracked the seal, drank, handed the bottle to Wolf. —Pretty good.
—Best. Costs a little more, but well worth it.
Wolf pulled onto the lot. —Okay, close your eyes. He took Wayne by the hand and led him into the booth, pushed him into a padded chair. A flourish of zippy music played. —All right, open up.
Wayne opened his eyes.
The set was flanked with high wooden bleachers. The bleachers were filled with screaming

kids. There were two wooden horses, and the scrims were painted with circus motifs. The children laughed and hollered. A man in a big game hunter's costume pulled the leashed Sponge Boy into view.

A banner unfurled along the top of the backdrop:

SPONGE BOY THE DRUNKEN DOG.

A clown joined the man in the hunter's suit. The man pulled the dog to a hitching post and tied the leash to it. He picked up a large, red, plastic bowl, took a liter of gin from inside his safari jacket and poured it into the bowl.

The clown watched, his clown eyes open wide.

As the man untied Sponge Boy's leash, the clown sneaked across the set, stole the bowl, and replaced it with an identical bowl. He filled the new bowl from a gasoline can.

—This dog, Wolf said, is bringing us more money than all the franchises did.

—I don't see it, Wayne said. It's just a bunch of kids.

—Parents buy. We're looking at merchandising, foreign rights. The fucking Japanese are crazy about that dog.

—And what if he dies? Wayne said.

Wolf pulled the car into their drive and put it in park. —Why would he die?

Bill was putting down landscape fabric in the flower bed.

—Every minute, Wayne said, everything alive takes that risk.

CONSTELLATION

—Put it on a greeting card, Wolf said. I wonder, given his inner strength, could anything kill him?

—He's that strong?

—He'll outlive us, I'll bet.

They walked toward the house. Wolf stopped and said something to Bill.

—Almost finished, Bill said.

—How do the plants get through? Wayne said.

Bill laughed. —You cut holes through the cloth when you put the plants down. Keep the weeds out.

—The plants aren't in there, Wayne said, but the weeds are?

—Seeds, I imagine, Bill said. He turned to Wolf. —Got the soil all turned. By hand.

He looked at Wayne. —That is, with a shovel. Turned it and fertilized it with the best you can get: fish heads.

—You know better, Wayne said.

—He's the gardener, Wolf said.

—Is no better, Bill said. This that I used is the best. Best in the whole world.

—A dog, Wayne said. I can't remember. It's a dog or is it an ox they'd kill and put there? Or maybe you figure it's best done with a man.

—Take it easy now, Wolf said.

Bill picked up the shovel and stepped away from Wayne. —There's nothing to be upset about.

Wayne stared evenly at Bill and straightened up to his full height. —I'm told, Wayne glanced at Wolf and back to Bill—you can catch the devil in a bag. But then it's said you're condemned to lug him on your back.

—You're getting yourself all worked up. Wolf said.

—Are you deaf as well as blind? Wayne said.

How long he was in the new bed, the hospital bed with restraints, restraints much stronger, tougher, than their woven fiber indicated, Wayne could not have said.

He was not sure when Wolf had ordered the bed.

From what he could see of his belted-down arms, it looked like they had not been feeding him intravenously. Perhaps, Wayne thought, Colleen had come and fed him, spooned broth into his open mouth. He could not remember.

He could not be sure.

Wolf came into the bedroom.

—Hello, Wayne said. Perhaps you'd consent to free me of these straps?

—You feel better now?

—Much better, Wayne said. Much relieved of my heavy burden.

—Came on you quick, Wolf said. Left quick too. Like the flu, I guess.

—Good analogy.

—So you're well enough to be up and around?

—Certainly.

—Free of your restraints?

—Absolutely.

—Umm, Wolf said. I worry that you might relapse, you know, if you see Bill.

—Who? Wayne said.

—You know, Farmer Bill.

CONSTELLATION

Wayne pulled against the restraints, tried to sit up, to break the straps. —It's as though God put an X on my brain.

—Don't make me get the syringe, Wolf said.

Wayne lay back. —Not necessary.

—Why can't you just leave him alone? He's harmless.

—You're a fool, Wayne said. Gardener as much a farmer as a fisherman, that rotting bastard Bill's no Bill.

—You're fucking nuts.

—Disguised himself to some evil end, boy.

—I had no idea you were this far gone. You'll never get out of those straps now.

—You'd best listen to me, Wayne said. Together maybe we can drive him off, but alone, you're finished.

—Never worry, Wayne. Never. Never happen.

—I understand your question, Wayne said. Don't think about it.

Wolf ran from the room.

Wayne laughed, laughed harder and harder, shaking in his restraints, and then began to weep. He wept for a long time.

When he woke up, there was a television set in the room. Wolf was there with the tv, the tv on a cart and on that cart with that tv, appeared to be a Sony or some Japanese make, there was a VCR. Wolf put a tape into the VCR and adjusted the set.

Sponge Boy came on the screen. He was riding in the bed of a big, red, American-made pick-up truck. The streets were lined with people. Mobs of people,

cheering people, and as Sponge Boy went by, the people threw things, pieces of plastic and metal, charcoal bricquets, vials of acid, cans of insecticide. Sponge Boy ate and drank the things that landed in the truck. The people cheered.
      Seemed like Wolf played the tape over and over.
      Seemed like Wolf was trying to get Wayne to say something. To agree to something.

      —Yes, Wayne said. All right. Whatever you say.
      —Just, Wolf said laughing.
      —Just let me out of the straps.
      Wolf had a grocery bag. He set it on the floor and took out a jar. —Now look close. You see?
      He held the jar in front of Wayne's face. Shook it gently.
      Wayne stared at the fluid. The grayish-white mass.
      Wolf held the jar at arm's length. —What an intricate and useless organ. Seat of our triumphs and griefs. He looked at Wayne. —Don't you agree?
      —Truer words, Wayne said.
      —Anyway, there's your proof. That's dead as dead gets.

      Wolf freed Wayne.
      —Shouldn't we at least shock him? Colleen said.
      —Not yet, Wolf said. Besides, I haven't got the equipment here.

CONSTELLATION

—It's as though my long nightmare is over, Wayne said. Often I dreamed I was driving a car with bad bearings. Jingling of the bed springs put me in mind of it, perhaps.

Wayne sprang from the bed and jogged around the room. He raced down the hall into his bedroom. He opened the closet, rummaged around, came out with his holstered .44. Wayne strapped on the holster, drew the gun, checked the cylinder.

—Never without you again, Baby, Wayne said.

Wolf made a deal with some sponsors, a chain of pet and pet supply stores, Wayne thought, to put some guests on the Sponge Boy Show. The guests, as Wayne understood it, were like Sponge Boy's friends, other animals that came to visit him.

Wayne did not know whether the animals had dialogue; the sponsors wanted it, but Wolf had some artistic problems with the idea. Of course the other animals were not allowed to eat burning tar or drink dry cleaning fluid.

And it was Wolf's show. This was not like TOTAL SECURITY; Wayne was effectively out of it now. Not that he was unhappy. As long as the .44 was strapped to him day and night, Wayne was happy.

He no longer watched the show. He didn't tell Wolf that. Mostly Wayne walked the streets, his .44 concealed by his long, black coat.

Japanese Monkey came to town. Japanese Monkey, a big star back in Japan, had his own show like Sponge Boy's although he did not get drunk or eat toxic materials, preferring, apparently, to act out scenes from the national literature and perform impressions and complicated magic tricks.

—Cultural differences, Wolf said. Anyway, this is the one to watch. Japanese tv is playing it live in Japan.

—Just this one? Colleen said.

—Who knows? Wolf said. Could be our opening into the all important Asian market. Wayne, watch this one.

Wolf was wearing a powder blue tuxedo and holding a bullwhip in one hand and a microphone in the other.

Sponge Boy was atop a painted drum.

—Our special guest, Wolf said, on his new American tour.

Japanese Monkey drove onto the set in a miniature black Cadillac. Sponge Boy, panting, hopped off the drum and chased the car, his tail wagging, his tongue hanging happily from his mouth. Japanese Monkey accelerated, made a quick U-turn, chased Sponge Boy in circles around the stage.

Wolf laughed, stepped in front of the car, his hands outstretched. —Okay, enough now.

Japanese Monkey sped up and rammed the car into Wolf's shins. Wolf screamed, jumped, leapt the length of the car.

The children in the studio audience laughed and applauded.

Wolf limped off stage.

Sponge Boy lay on his side.

CONSTELLATION

Japanese Monkey did a series of flips across the stage, stood facing the audience, stretched his arms, took a deep bow. He did another series of flips, exited the stage, and returned wearing a traditional kimono and samurai swords.

Japanese Monkey bowed to the audience and to Sponge Boy. Sponge Boy stood up. Japanese Monkey drew his swords, swirled them in a flourish, cut off Sponge Boy's whiskers. Sponge Boy whined, stepped backwards.

Wolf walked onto the stage with a .45 automatic and shot Japanese Monkey in the head.

Wayne opened the front door. Wolf was on the stoop, a grocery bag in each hand.

—This ape, Wayne said, will be our doom.

Wolf brushed past him. —I've had a shit day.

—A shit day, Wolf called from the kitchen, and I forgot I invited some potential sponsors over, so don't start in with me.

Wayne went into the kitchen. Wolf pulled on a chef's hat and apron and picked up a cookbook.

Wayne saw the produce on the counter: lettuce, carrots, radishes, red onions, cabbage. —Can I help?

—Make the salad, Wolf said. But be careful not to cut yourself. All we need now is blood in the bowl.

The sponsors, a man from a lumber yard and a man who owned a petting zoo, had not arrived at six.

Wolf stirred up a pitcher of martinis, remarking that perhaps the guests would be late, as was, after all, the fashion, and after the tensions of the day, the hosts would do well to have a pop before the guests arrived. Colleen and Wayne assented and held out their glasses while Wolf poured. Wayne tried to make a toast, raised his glass and started in, but he could not for the life of him remember what he was trying to say. Colleen did not want to wait all night for a cocktail, so they forgot about the toast.

The telephone rang; Wolf went into the den to get it.

He was back in a minute, the chef's cap balled up in his fists. —They aren't coming. Goddamn it, they aren't fucking interested. Now, of a sudden, out of the fucking blue, when I've got everything preparing in the kitchen, this meal, the feast I have planned for weeks, they call up and say they are no longer interested in a business relationship with me, with fucking Wolf fucking Murphy.

He threw the hat on the floor and jumped up and down on it. The hat slid out from under him; Wolf nearly lost his footing.

—I will bury them. I will bury them. I will, mark my fucking words, bury them.

Something scratched at the front door.

—It's that dog, Wayne said, working his nails upon our entry.

—We don't have a dog, Colleen said.

Wolf ran to the door and flung it open.

Bill stood on the stoop. He was holding a broom. —Just give her the old cleanup. He winked. —Make her look nice and pretty.

—Come in, Wolf said. All you and yours are welcome here this night.

CONSTELLATION

—Mine? Bill said.

—Your family, Wolf said.

Bill laughed. —None that I know of, anyway. He pushed his baseball cap back on his head. —I'm finished here, and I'm free for the evening.

—Join us, Wolf said.

Bill looked around the room. —This is no joke?

Wolf waved him inside. —Come, come.

Colleen handed Bill a martini. —The more the merrier.

Wayne shook his head.

Wolf jabbed Wayne in the ribs with his elbow. —Aren't you gonna greet our guest?

—Where are your manners? Colleen said.

—You invite trouble on yourselves, Wayne said.

—C'mon now, Wolf said. He looked at Bill. —You have to excuse him.

—He's sick, Colleen said.

Wolf tapped his forehead. —Not quite right, you know?

—Kind words won't help you, Wayne said. There's no protection in the air.

Wolf smiled at Bill. —No offense.

Bill ate the olive from his martini. —None taken. He wiped his mouth with his sleeve. —Very decent of you, inviting the help for a drink and all. Usually this sort of thing only happens at Christmas.

—Do we have any finger food? Wayne said.

Colleen sat at one end of the table. Wolf's place was at the other. Wayne slumped in his chair, looking at the roses in the crystal vase. Bill sat across from Wayne, his linen napkin tucked into the collar of his work shirt.

Wolf circled the table, ladling soup from a tureen into the diners' bowls. —I should have hired somebody. A waiter.

—The cooking I don't mind, Wolf said. All the greatest chefs are men. But it would lend some ambiance to our gathering to have a tuxedoed waiter provide us service.

He sat down. —Soup's on. Enjoy.

Bill slurped his soup. —Damned good.

—So I sit at your left hand, Wayne said, while he sits at your right.

—You're still the right hand for me, Colleen said.

—What the hell is in this soup? Wayne said.

—Put off this grief, Wayne. 'Tis unmanly, Wolf said. Better to spend our time practicing for the real dangers of this world.

Wayne sobbed, his salad plate pushed aside, his head on the table.

—Always this or that, Colleen said, draining her glass. —Wolf, get another bottle.

—Yeah, Wolf said. Drink more.

—Now there's somebody using the old brain pan, Bill said.

Wayne sat up straight and glared at Bill. —So you'll tell me how to live as though you descended to my level with that in mind?

—Sharp words, is that it? Bill stood up.

Wolf came in with a liter of vodka from the

CONSTELLATION

kitchen. —Sit friend, and I beg you, take no offense. For as clear as his features, all can see my poor uncle is mad.

—Mad Wayne, Colleen said. Off his nut.

—Maybe you think I'm simple, Bill said. People want to see us farmers in one way, sentimentalize us as they sentimentalize everything that belongs to the past, everything that's almost gone. But remember the boredom, the daily chores, how we longed to be free of that land.

Wolf brought in a tray and served seafood cocktails. —This was supposed to come first. He shrugged, picked up the vodka, took a slug. —You know how it is.

—Should have told me, Farmer Bill said. I'd have got you some fish.

—Farmer or fisherman? Mad Wayne said.

—He's mad. We never said it, but now it's out in the open. The naked truth, Drunk Colleen said. She spooned into her cocktail.

—I left the farm at an early age, Farmer Bill said, and went to sea. Fished and fucked and fought my way around the world as only a sailor can.

He winked at Colleen.

She blushed and licked her spoon. —Perhaps you'll tell us all about it.

Mad Wayne sang:

> This world is a carnal house,
> And a charnel house as well.
> Some days it strikes me beautiful,
> Others it seems sure hell.

—Life is so interesting, Drunk Colleen said. Once I was an innocent girl with skin like cream.

Now—now, perhaps the flesh is a bit different.

Wolf went into the kitchen.
—I wonder, Mad Wayne said, does he have a fortress, or more properly, a fortified house, hidden somewhere in the hills?
—You never really know a person, Drunk Colleen said. I lived with Bob all those years, and frankly, I never knew the half of it.
She threw back her head and laughed. —And this one, she pointed to Wayne, —is crazy. How much good do you think he is?
Wolf set a covered silver tray on the table.
—All right, he said, here's the *chef d'oeuvre*.
Wolf pulled the lid off the tray. A roasted monkey with an apple in its mouth lay surrounded by carrots and potatoes. Wolf looked around the table at the assemblage. —Who wants a paw? He laughed. —Hell, I guess there's one here for each of us. The meat, I'm told, closest to the bone, is the sweetest.
Mad Wayne leapt from his chair and flung his napkin onto his plate. —You presume to mock me, sir?
Wolf flashed the carving knife in front of Wayne's face. —You may be mad, but don't force me to give you a lesson in manners.
—Have your eyes left your head? Mad Wayne said. Yet you shot the ape well enough. It's been said, been well reported, something about a blind man with an arrow, or perhaps it was a monkey with a typewriter.
—Sit down, Honey, Drunk Colleen said. Have a drink. For Christ's sake, have a drink.

CONSTELLATION

Mad Wayne pointed to Bill. —Can't any of you see who has come to sup at my living table?
—I'm terribly sorry about this, Wolf said. He pulled a sap from his jacket pocket. —I wish we could somehow turn this to the good; maybe have somebody study him and find a cure.
—I took the measure of the man myself, Drunk Colleen said. Not much to look at.
Wolf stepped behind Wayne.

Wayne opened his eyes and saw the pattern, the tiny blue and pink and gold flowers, in his plate. His face was pressed against the china and his head ached. Wayne clenched and unclenched his right fist, slid the hand into his shirt, and eased the long-barrelled .44 onto his lap.
Wayne sat up, cocked the pistol, and sang:

Side by side is my promise,
And never shall we part.
 Should any 'tempt to cleave us
He'll learn your fearsome art.

He levelled the pistol at Wolf.
Wolf looked at Wayne, nodded, continued eating.
—Be careful with that, Farmer Bill said.
—Fuck off, Mad Wayne said.
Drunk Colleen took a slice of meat from the platter.
—How sweet, Mad Wayne said, that the dead feed the living this night.
—Nonsense, Wolf said.

—It's always the way it is, Drunk Colleen said. Eat and you'll feel better.

The devil was upon me,
And I did not give a damn,
Till he put it in my ear,
That I was only half a man,

Wayne sang.

—I imagine the little people out there, entertained by us, happy with what they're getting, left alone with a vision of an America long lost, Wolf said. And now you have to take out a gun and try to spoil it all.

—Shame, Fisherman Bill said.

Mad Wayne lay the pistol on the table, his hand still on the grip. —I think sometimes, he nodded deeply, —that we made something in this world. At a cost, it's true, but what comes without a cost? If I could reconcile myself to that making, to that damn cost, my troubles would surely leave me, disappear into the air, I think.

—You give the air a lot of credit, Farmer Bill said.

—I know, Mad Wayne said.

—You need to let go the past, Wolf said.

—That's enough out of you, Drunk Colleen said.

—Let go, let go, let go, and shut up, Mad Wayne said.

—Each day a new beginning, Wolf said. A new birth.

—Huh. Uh huh. Huh, Mad Wayne said.

—Build up a force, Fish Farmer Bill said, a force that doesn't just let go, a force that tears it away.

CONSTELLATION

—Dead bastard, Mad Wayne said.
—Fuck off, Drunk Colleen said.
—On, Dead Farmer Bill said.
—Indeed, Mad Wayne said, it's as though everything hangs, floats, and when I try to touch it, it floats away. Hangs there. Hangs more than floats. Just bounces off, bumps away.
—Get down to earth, Farmer Bill said.
—Come up for air, Fisherman Bill said.
—Push off that weight, Farm Fisher Bill said.
—Hangs, Wolf laughed, when you feel the rope, you'll know the weight.
—That's right, Drunk Colleen said. You only really know the weight when you're on the bottom.
—Yes, Mad Wayne said, when I am endungeoned my own hair I'll weave. First, to make myself a shirt, and in time a shroud, and finally a rope.
—Good, Dead Fish Farmer Bill said. Very nice to have a relaxing hobby. He pushed the platter toward Wayne. —Now eat, and you'll feel better.
Mad Wayne raised the gun from the table.
—Will I die at the hands of my ghoulish enemies?
—Fuck, fuck, fuck, Drunk Colleen said.
Mad Wayne fell weeping to the floor.

Wayne awoke as Colleen was pulling the tablecloth off him the next morning.
—We thought it best not to move you, she said.
—You don't, don't worry.
Colleen chuckled. —I hope that's the last we'll see of this act. Wolf was hurt, the way you ruined his party.

—Is it you? Wayne said.
—Yes.
—It's you?
—Yes, Wayne. It's me, your little Colleen, your little Love Bird.
—I don't believe it's you, Wayne said. It's someone else who is controlling my thoughts. Until I discover the first cause of my troubles, I can offer little defense.
—Don't you want to get up off the floor, Honey?
—The best I can offer is refusal. No longer will I be a passive instrument and broadcast the thoughts of others. I now silence myself forthwith until my enemy reveals himself.

Wolf slapped cologne on his face, capped the bottle, set it in his desk drawer. —Cost me a ton of yen to put out the story their fucking chimp got greased in an accident and couldn't be recovered. Who knew how serious they took him? A state funeral *in absentia*. Man, it's unbelievable.
Wayne sat, knocking his knees together and rolling his head around, in the visitor's chair.
—Cat got your tongue? Wolf said. Anyway, it's all fine now. You won't talk; I don't blame you. Words huh? Fuck em. But you're still part of the network.

The kids were in the bleachers and Wolf's new assistant, Desiree, a shapely, red-headed young

CONSTELLATION

woman, was showing cartoons on the monitor as a warm up.
 Wolf tugged at the front of Wayne's shirt. —Get it straight now. C'mon, look sharp.
 He pushed Wayne into a cage, a cage on painted wheels, its floor covered with straw like an antique circus wagon.
 Wolf reached through the bars and pulled frantically at Wayne's lapels. —Keep it straight for God's sake. You're about to go on.
 Wayne, confused, tried to climb the bars of the cage.
 —The sign, Wolf said.
 Wayne dropped from the bars and stared at Wolf.
 Desiree came off stage, grabbed the wagon's tongue and pulled the wagon toward the stage.
 —We're on in three, someone shouted.
 Wayne fell to the floor, stood up, braced himself against the bars, and straightened the sign that hung from a chain around his neck.
 The sign read JAP MONKEY.
 —We'll get you a seltzer bottle later, Wolf said. Just hang on the bars for now.

 Wayne found he could not remember everything—all the jeers, paper and rocks and vegetables thrown, buckets of water dumped, electrical shocks, fire extinguishers sprayed—all the pelting and pummeling merged together. After each show, Colleen pushed him into a shower stall at the studio and scrubbed him down. At some point they gave him a vinyl monkey suit, the black fur colored on the

65

material. The suit helped, but it didn't breathe.

Then it was over.
—A joke's a joke, Wolf said. The kids are bored with you.
Wayne had just suited up and got into the cage. He stood there, his mouth open, hands clasped on the barred door. He tried to swing the door shut.
Wolf caught the door and held it open.
—Come on now. You've been written out of the show.
Wayne pulled, pulled as hard as he could on the door, but Wolf was stronger.
—Okay, Wolf said. Come out, but hang up the suit. Maybe we'll be able to use you again later.
Wayne stepped slowly down from the cage.
—Careful, Wolf said.
—Don't worry, Wayne said, brushing his vinyl-covered chest. —It's like a second skin to me.

Wayne hung around the studio. Wolf let him sweep up, clean the bathroom, empty the wastebaskets. After a few weeks, Wayne asked when he'd be back on the show.
—It's hopeless, Wolf said. Jap Monkey's as dead as the Toltecs.
Wayne dropped his broom. —The only word I know is no.
—Look, Wolf said, I'll give you the keys to the company condo. Cool off.

CONSTELLATION

Wayne watched the green-lighted dial on the huge, rounded short wave. —This, he said, is the most important machine. People don't know how important this machine is.

No one else was in the room.

—I am over one hundred and twenty-five years old, Wayne said, and I owe it all to this.

—Yet I could be described, accurately, as a figure of palpable despair.

Wayne wore a walkman at the table and jerked back and forth, apparently in time with some music, in his chair. Wolf sat down at the head of the table, poured himself a glass of whiskey from a cut glass decanter, passed the decanter to Colleen.

She filled her glass. —Hard day?

—Hard life, Wolf said. Look at my partner.

Wayne's head bobbed. His eyes were shut.

—He's fine, Colleen said.

—Where's Bill?

—Who knows?

—I wish he'd stay around the house, Wolf said. I might need him to do something.

Colleen shrugged. —Eat. You'll feel better.

—Yeah, Wolf said. These fucking franchisees never let up.

—I thought you were done with them.

—They filed another suit. It's trash, simple harassment. Wolf filled his glass. —They're jealous. They see Sponge Boy going through the roof, and they all want a piece, the venal fucks.

—Let your lawyers take care of it, Colleen

said. I don't want you to worry yourself sick.
—Yeah, Wolf said. He shook his head. —What a bunch of geeks and hicks. Ought to have them all over here for dinner and make em wear those HELLO I'M BLANK stickers. Sticker em and then blow em all up.
Colleen held up the platter. —Have another pork chop; you'll feel better.
—Just when things were getting in line at the station. Wolf forked a couple chops onto his plate. —Did you realize we have thirty full time employees now? I just announced the most productive employees stay; the rest are history. It was great, like throwing coins to urchins.
Wayne poured himself a glass of gin. Colleen motioned him to take off the headphones.
—Eat, Honey, Colleen said.
—Eat? Later. Wayne nodded to Wolf. —At least he's out of the house. I can hear him banging some damn thing out in the garage.
—Have a chop, Baby, Colleen said.
Wayne sniffed the meat.
—I told him to get the riding mower going, Wolf said. Hell, he can fix anything.
—There's a funny scent to it, Wayne said. He stood up. —How long have you had it there in the cooler?
—Nothing wrong with this, Wolf said.
—And the dog? Wayne said.
—Good food. Eat, Wolf said. Eat while you can.
—You feed in peace.
—Sooner than you think all this could be gone. Obsolete. Nothing but a memory. How's that make you feel, by the way?

CONSTELLATION

—Eat, drink. Wayne sat down. —Tomorrow die. Something like that? He put his hand on the butt of the .44 inside his shirt. —What of our hound?
—Still first in the ratings, given our unique market position.
—I'd be happy to make you something else, Colleen said.
—No doubt, Wayne snapped.
—That's enough, Wolf said. Why are you so interested in our star?
—Get him in this house nights. That'll keep our wanderer outside.
—I don't want any dog barking all night, Colleen said. And they smell, especially when they're wet. After the rain. Spare me.
—Oh, they smell, Wayne said. They smell and know long before us. And your wanderer fears they'll scent him, and he knows to stay away.
—I got a thorn in my side, Wolf said, and you want to stir up my dog. He threw his napkin in his plate. —I have real problems, not this shit.
He got up from the table.

Wayne walked along the privacy fence in the back yard. He peered at the ground. Wayne stopped beneath a black walnut tree, squatted, ran his hand along a root and the earth.
—Lose something?
Wayne looked up.
Bill stood, a hoe resting on his shoulder.
—You think you can swing that hard enough to sever me?
—What?

—Try me, Wayne said. I'll show you what fucking substance is.
—Now. Bill leaned the hoe against the tree trunk. —You got the wrong idea about me, Friend.
—And you'll give me the right one?
—What did you lose? I'll help you look.
Wayne stroked the tree root. —I like nature.
Bill shrugged.
—I like to think about it. Trees. Flowers. That kind of thing.
—Maybe you'd like a turn in the garden, Bill said.
Wayne got up and walked toward the back gate.
—You want out? Bill said. Suppose they gave it to you, your proverbial forty acres and a mule. You'd starve before the paperwork came through.

—Where did you find him this time? Wolf said.
—The doctor gave him something, Colleen said. He's supposed to sleep for awhile.
—Like he doesn't do enough of that.
—I know I shouldn't bother you at work, Colleen said. It's just when I see him strapped to those stretchers, I get so upset.
—It's okay, Ma.
—Once he gets it out of his system, I'm sure he'll be fine, just like before.
—I'll look in on him.
—He was down at the river in that abandoned grotto. You know, where the seminary used to be. He could have been out for a walk, just out for a walk like

CONSTELLATION

anybody else, except for the bathrobe and the gun. Well, when he wouldn't talk to the policemen—
—He's home now. Don't worry.
Wolf went upstairs. Wayne lay in bed, his arms crossed beneath his head. He was staring at the textured ceiling.
—I thought you'd be asleep, Wolf said.
—I was looking for that tree, Wayne said. I can readily call it to mind, as real as though I'd seen it in a painting. Low-limbed, sturdy. A tree that could easily bear some weight.
—That's fine, Wolf said. But you know, we agreed that if you weren't at the studio, you'd stay around the house. You know how Colleen worries about your straying off.
—It seems unduly difficult to find the right one, Wayne said.
—How about, Wolf said, I buy you a tree. One of those little ones, you know, seedling or sapling or what the fuck you call it. You can plant it out in the yard and water it, watch it grow. Hell, after awhile you might want to prune it, you know, shape it, like, like ah, those Jap ones they got.
—Maybe if I find what I'm looking for, Wayne said, I can make a couch of it.
—Sure, Wolf said.
—Or a stump end table.
—Sure. Bill could maybe help you.
Wayne sat up and screamed.
—Oops, Wolf said.

—You stay outside, Wolf said. Do something in back.

71

—Whatever you say, Bill said. Believe me, that lift will work fine.

Wolf pressed some bills into Bill's hand.

—Yeah, thanks. You did great.

A wall-mounted light went on over the living room closet door. Wolf opened the door. Colleen pulled open the cage and wheeled the wheelchair-bound Wayne out of the elevator.

—It's so convenient, she said.

—I didn't think he could do it, Wolf said. Right through the closets. Hell of a job.

—You'll want your rug, Colleen said. She tucked a heavy blanket around Wayne.

—Trees, Wayne said.

—That's right, Wolf said. You'll see plenty.

Colleen wheeled Wayne to Wolf's Cadillac convertible. Wolf lifted Wayne into the back seat, folded up the chair, and put it in the trunk.

Colleen sat beside Wayne, her arm around his shoulder, while Wolf, chauffeur-like, drove.

—Maybe we'll hit a rest stop and put the top down if he's not too cold, Wolf said.

—Look, Darling, Colleen said, we're out of the city. Way past the beltway. She laughed. —It's just too bad we couldn't get out a few weeks ago, when the leaves were still on the trees.

—Best colors in years this year, I heard, Wolf said.

Wayne coughed. —The sky is gray as slate. Slate gray, I believe is the term.

Colleen laughed. —Don't be silly. Slate is black.

—Gray, Wayne said.

—In school the blackboards were black, Dearest. We didn't need the sisters to tell us that.

—Gray, Wayne said.

CONSTELLATION

—You're being obstinate, Sweetheart. The black blackboards were made of slate.

—Clean slate is a good thing, huh? Wolf said. Every morning the sun comes up, and you've got a clean slate. Somebody told me that once.

—That's enough about somebody, Colleen said. Somebody isn't with us now.

—Not a leaf on a tree, Wayne said, and look at the snow in those fields.

—No snow, Wolf said. It's a white plant.

—That's clover, Honey, Colleen said.

Wayne drew his legs up to his chest. —It's the gray sky, the snow, it's the dead trees, it's like the land of the dead.

—The land of the dead, the fucking land of the dead, Colleen said. Can't we go anywhere we don't end up in the land of the dead?

She pulled a pint of aquavit out of her purse, cracked the seal, took a long drink. —Want a pop, Wolf?

—It's illegal to drink in a moving vehicle in this state, Wayne said.

—Our laws are necessarily reactive, imposed to correct or mitigate a preexisting problem, Colleen said. They are, therefore, artificial and unnatural.

Colleen took a drink.

Wayne hyperventilated.

—If you prefer something proactive, Colleen said, have the Chinese lock you down for awhile. See how you prefer that.

Wolf turned and glanced at Wayne. —Something to think about.

—Put me out of your thoughts, Wayne said. All will be easier for you if you are able to do that. Put me away, far away, so far away that to you I am nothing.

—Okay, Colleen said. Say no more.
—All is forgotten, Wolf said.
—That will make my mission so much easier, Wayne said, knowing that you will not not be forced to witness the suffering which has been preordained for me.
—Oh, Jesus Christ! Colleen said.

—Well, Colleen said, it was in the early spring, the kind of spring we used to have before the volcano in Asia kicked up all that dust in the air and ruined our weather for good, when everything started moist, the gray sky alternating with the sunshine, the melting snow and the mud, the gentle rain and the water running in the gutters, dripping musically from the rooftops and more sun, each drop a prism, even the oil sheen in the streets, rainbows atop the running water, and the birds coming out, the grass springing back green, green everywhere, the birds back from their winter's migration, and the smell, the smell of the fresh earth, the water, the plants returning to life, the breeze always fresh, at last, the windows, the closed-up houses opened from the long winter's enclosure with its stale scents of tobacco and wet wool, dry heat, cooking, all purged as easily and gently as the curtain blowing and billowing in the breeze.
—People felt free—freed of the heavy coats and boots and hats, free to walk outside bareheaded in the sun, to bicycle, to run, it seemed like everyone, the whole city, was outside. The restaurants put tables in their courtyards and the ice cream shops that had sold pumpkins in October and wreaths and trees in December reopened for their true, their only genuine,

CONSTELLATION

purpose. Of course they met; they had known each other, seen each other, he and she, at school, at the university. They knew each other to say hello; they had a class together, and she felt perhaps they watched each other a little, noticed each other, as young people will when their eyes are open and it is spring and nature takes its inevitable and circular course, generation in and generation out.

—She was walking across the campus, her sweater tied around her waist, in blue jeans and a white cotton blouse, and a necklace of worked turquoise and silver. There was a party that night, a floor party in her dorm, not on her floor, but she had friends on that floor and they thought she would be there.

—She wasn't so sure.

—A shy girl, more interested in her work, her studies, than in this party, or any party. Oh, she went out. She had friends. She loved to dance and wasn't afraid of a drink or a cigarette or a boy, any boy, but this afternoon, as she walked, she had not made up her mind, not yet, about her plans for the evening. It was a Friday, a Friday in the spring. She had the whole weekend, she had her whole life in front of her that day as she walked in the sun, across the campus, her feet in Mexican sandals.

—The boy, this boy in our story, came up behind her, ran around her, passed her by. She was startled for a moment as he went by. She noticed his shorts. She noticed his sweatshirt. His hair. His shoes, she noticed the brand and model of shoes he was wearing.

—Of course, she did some running too.

—All this noticing, remember she was a young girl, quick and quick-minded, happened in a flash, in the same moment that she was startled, she took him in.

—And he her, apparently, for he turned around and apologized as he jogged backwards beside her, apologized repeatedly, for having startled her, for not having been more careful, for having come upon her suddenly.

—Not a shy girl, she, but she flushed, flushed for a moment and looked down at her toes in her sandals, waiting, waiting as he ran in place, to say exactly the right thing to him, and she looked up and smiled and said, It's you.

—They talked and she went on to the library, and he back to his room to shower and change and go out and get a bottle of wine and bread and cheese and ripe pears and a flower, a red flower, and he found her in the library where she was reading, a wisp of hair on her forehead, her graceful fingers turning the pages langorously, and he was there with all the things he had got, not in a wicker basket, but in a plain brown grocery bag he had rolled easily at the top and now held easily in his left hand.

—And will you, he said after he had said some other things, some things she responded to, some things she hung on at the time, and will you, he said, come out with me for a little while this evening?

—For a little while this evening.

—These words seemed to her—something—quaint, quiet—muted—speaking more than themselves, telling her something, showing her something about him that perhaps he wanted her—her and perhaps no one else—to see.

—She breathed deeply. All right, she said. She nodded and smiled and said, all right.

—He leaned in toward her as she stood up,

CONSTELLATION

pushing her chair behind her with the backs of her knees, and for a moment, a second, she pivoted a little, maybe so little he did not notice it, she pivoted as though he were about to offer her his arm, and she was about to take it, and arm in arm they would walk out the doors and down the broad marble steps of the library for all to see. She followed him out, he turning to hold each of the double doors for her as she walked, not aloof and tall, but smiling, bemused, from the building.

—On the landing, after the doors, before the first step, he offered her his arm, and she took it.

—How long had she been inside?

—It had seemed only minutes, but now, as they descended the staircase to the pavement, the violet evening was falling and stars began to blink in the dusky sky. The moon was rising, full and silver and luminous, and the omnipresent breeze was still gentle and cool, as if a long night, a night long awaited were softly evolving before her eyes.

—She smiled and said, Where are we headed?

—I know the place, he said.

—They walked and he put his arm around her, gently, and they walked the quiet pavement beneath the antique street lamps, and they saw people on their stoops, children running in the yards, the quiet summer-slow prowl of passing cars. Inside houses lights were on, and people sat on porches or in living rooms talking and laughing quietly, playing cards, watching television.

—After they had gone a long way, they reached, and she knew it, knew as they arrived that they were arriving at their destination, a high wooded hill with a winding path to its peak.

—Could they have skipped up the hill? Or was

it only that they seemed, to her, so light, so quick and easy that they bore no weight, not the weight of the parcel, not even the weight of their bodies. She seemed to be floating, and he floating with her, as they reached the summit, where he spread a cloth on the ground and unpacked his bag and lay their humble supper before her.

—They ate and drank looking down at the lights of the city spread before them and at the moon and stars above them and this night, this warm, quiet, violet night on the hill, this night that seemed theirs as though everything else in grasp were but a prop, a stage on which he and she acted together as one alone.

—Is he asleep? Wolf said.
—Christ, I hope so, Colleen said.
Wayne was bent nearly double in the back seat, his head twisted to one side, eyes closed, mouth opened.
Colleen shook her head. —How may times do I have to tell him that fucking story?

Wayne paced in front of Wolf's desk at the studio.
—And? Wolf said.
—And? And? And I think I'm entitled to some input. I'm your partner, Wolf.
—You've been sick.
—I'm as well, Wayne said, as I'm going to be.
Wolf put a bottle of vodka and two glasses on his desk. —Okay, sit down. He poured vodka into the

CONSTELLATION

glasses. —I'll explain what's up.

Wayne picked up a glass. —What happened to your face?

A running sore the size of a quarter beneath Wolf's right eye.

—This? Some kind of skin thing. I think I caught it from the dog.

Wayne nodded.

—Doctor gave me some stuff yesterday, Wolf said, that could clear it right up.

Wayne sipped his drink, sat down.

—If this new balm can't handle it, I'm thinking about a patch. Not, you know, an eye patch, but one of those bandage patches.

—Like an oval shape? Wayne said.

—Yeah, those tan ones. Wolf poured vodka into Wayne's glass. —Top us off, and let's get to it. I know you've been patient, and I know you have plenty of great ideas, and I didn't want to bother you while you were sick, but things aren't quite as rosy as you seem to believe.

—No, Wayne said.

—I had to file restaining orders on all the franchisees, their employees, and families. Those bastards were driving by the house and upsetting Mother. Just because we stomped the candy asses in court, fair and square.

—Around the house? Wayne said. Where the hell was I?

—You were catatonic. Let's have a look out back.

Wolf gulped his drink and ushered Wayne out of the office. They walked past the sound stage. Wayne's cage stood empty in the corner.

—Sponge Boy's still bringing in revenue, Wolf

said. But some fucking parents' group is leading a crusade against him and the health and recovery people won't sell us any more programming. I tried for some evangelists at the Vegas convention, but even they won't touch us now. All I got were some foreign language soaps, and the plums were taken. The big boys got Spanish; we're left with Latvian and Indonesian.

—All the more reason for me to be developing some programming, Wayne said.

—With what for start up? We need cash, cash infusion, to stay liquid.

Wayne stopped beside the fire door. —Are we going under?

—I don't know.

—Poverty again? Fuck, again? Does it ever end?

Wolf put his arm on Wayne's shoulder. —It's peaks and valleys. I knew that going in.

Wolf guided Wayne out the steel doors to the alley. Interns were loading a refrigerated truck with boxes from skids. The white cardboard boxes were crisscrossed with metal bands. The sides of the boxes were printed with black writing in some alphabet Wayne could not identify: Arabic, Farsi, Khmer? Blood dripped from the boxes and formed small pools on the asphalt.

—We in the blood business? Wayne said.

—Blood? Wolf laughed. —No, though time was we could've made a killing there. This is meat. I had to make a deal with some South Americans I know.

—We're not in dope?

Wolf shook his head. —We're desperate, not suicidal. This is Argentine beef.

CONSTELLATION

—But the writing—
—From the packing plant. Spanish, for all we know. Anyway, it could have been packed anywhere. You, lift with your knees. I don't want any worker's comp shit here.
—What are we doing with it?
—Fast money. Knees, damn it! I know a guy with a chain of restaurants, and if this goes well, we've got a toehold in food distribution.
—Toehold, Wayne said. That's something.
—People have to eat. We'll push this stuff as chemical free, feature it on a montage—nature, fields, rivers—with some public domain classical music in the background. OUR EVOLVING WORLD—you want work, Wayne, you're unit producer. Get me pictures of nature. Use magazines, cigarette ads. This will cost us nothing.
—Yes, Wayne nodded. Producer.
—We've got man's best friend. Now it's time for some bovine betties.

Wayne stood in front of the full-length mirror in his bathroom. —There's nothing wrong with me.
—There's nothing wrong with me.
—There's nothing wrong with me that someone can't fix.
Someone pounded on the door.
Wayne stepped back. —Come.
Wolf opened the door and held up a stuffed manila envelope. —It's here.
—What?
—C'mon.
Wayne followed Wolf to the living room.

Wolf took a cassette out of the envelope, shoved it into the VCR, adjusted the set.

The screen showed a plain of dry grass with a few broadly spreading trees and a mountain range in the background. A strange bird called loudly. A herd of antelope ran onto the plain. In the lower left hand corner of the screen, a couple of lions trailed the herd.

Wayne sat down on the couch.

The antelopes ran faster.

The lions picked up speed, moved toward the edge of the herd, cut off the mother antelope and her kid.

The herd kept moving. One lion feinted at the mother. She pulled back, dodged around the predator. The other lion pounced on the kid and brought it down.

The mother followed the herd as the first lion trotted over to the downed kid.

Bill came in. He was carrying a concrete lawn toad. —Wolf—

—Sit down, Wolf said.

Wayne skidded over and Bill gently set the toad on the carpet and sat down beside Wayne.

More lions joined the two hunters. They encircled the kill, eating, their muzzles dripping with blood.

—This is incredible, Wolf said.

Bill shrugged. —Happens every day. More than once a day, maybe.

—In the right season, Wayne said. I think there's some seasonal aspect to these hunts.

—Feast or famine. Wolf said. Nature designs that in.

—So long as neither lasts too long, Wayne said.

CONSTELLATION

  —Nature has a design for that as well, Bill said.
  The scene shifted to a muddy, brown river. Rhinos bathed in the water. A gigantic crocodile slithered up the bank.
  —That reptile will be looking for something, Bill said.
  —Eating machines, Wolf said. I read an article.
  Wayne went upstairs. He opened his bedroom closet and took out a bulky, loose, uneven roll of butcher's paper and carried it to the living room.
  The crocodile was eating—something—a bloody mess with some fur or maybe feathers.
  Wayne unrolled a portion of the paper. Pictures of mountains, rivers, lakes, rock formations, and fields were pasted to the roll. Beneath each picture was scribbled the name and date of the magazine it had been clipped from.
  —Shhh, Wolf said. He motioned to the screen.
  Buzzards were eating a wildebeest.
  —I got them all, Wayne said. Just like you told me.
  —That's great, Bill said.
  —How do you splice them in? Wayne said.
  —Where? Wolf said.
  —For OUR EVOLVING WORLD.
  Wolf paused the tape. —This isn't for us. This is a promo. We're going on safari for vacation next year.
  —To Africa? Wayne said.
  —Not sure, Bill said. We're waiting for a tape from an outfit in Alaska.
  —I'm pretty impressed with this, Wolf said.

—It's something, Bill said. But you haven't seen Alaska yet.

Wayne rolled up the paper. —Let me know when you need this.

—We will, Wolf said. Listen, Wayne, why don't you come with us this time?

—I don't know, Wayne said.

—Best thing for you, Bill said. Get out in the wild.

Wayne stopped arranging the paper and looked Bill full in the face. —You think it's best, eh?

—It'll be great, Wolf said. We all go out to Africa or someplace with tents and food and booze and guns. Hell, this is what you've been needing all along.

—Sure, Bill said. Take a few risks, that'll get you on target.

—You take risks? Wayne said.

Bill said, —Taken the ones I had to. Ever been in the tropics? I'll tell you this: It's not quite like your picture shows. There's the heat. You wake up wet, you sweat all day, you sleep the sleep you can, sweating it all the way through. That's old news. Insects and scorpions, yeah, they're there. But I'll tell you what got me. It's the noise. You ever have to be so quiet, so still, you were more than silent? That's when it's the hardest, when you really have to do it, and that's when you notice that noise never stops. You crouch there in the jungle, the forest, they call it, and that name's as apt as any, and it seems that everything is moving, the branches, the leaves, the water drip, drip, drip. Drop of water hits a leaf like an explosion, and you want to jump, boy, like it went off inside you. Then the birds always calling and at twilight they come in, those birds, the sky black with

CONSTELLATION

them, and they set down in the trees to roost, more birds than you've ever seen, and you're there, beneath that canopy, beneath the anarchy of a thousand tropical birds singing.

—You wouldn't want to miss that, Wolf said.

—Maybe we could film it, Wayne said.

—I've an idea there, Bill said. You get this guy with a kayak and a computer and send him to the ends of the earth.

—Adventures, Wayne said.

—Yeah, Wolf said. Claim he's doing a study. Get a big, good-looking guy.

Wayne and Bill carried a battered wooden fold-down desk into the living room.

—Colleen, Wayne yelled.

—Put her in the corner there, Bill, Wayne said.

Bill picked up the desk.

Wayne walked over to him. —I'll help.

—I got her, Bill said. He set the desk in the corner.

—Colleen, Wayne shouted.

A door upstairs slammed.

—That'll be her, Bill said. He brushed his hands against each other. —Women. He shook his head.

Colleen, in a black dress, descended the staircase. A rosary hung loosely from her right hand. —I was at my prayers.

—Prayers? Since when? Wayne said.

—We have to pray for the conversion of Russia, Colleen said.

—I thought they had converted, Bill said. To something, anyway.

—There will be many signs and wonders, Colleen said. All this is well known. But beware: These signs and wonders are false.

—How do you know what's not false then? Wayne said.

—If you know the truth, Colleen said, the truth will be revealed.

—She's got her wimple on tonight, boy, Bill said. He winked.

—Watch your fucking mouth, fucker, Wayne said.

Bill put his hands in the air. —No offense, pard.

—Anyway, Wayne said, what do you think of it?

He guided Colleen over to the desk.

—A box, she said.

—That's real wood, Bill said. Cherry.

—Yes, Colleen said. Wood. A wooden box.

Wayne opened the desk. —It folds down. See?

—A box that opens and closes, Colleen said. And all for me. How very thoughtful. What a wonderful gift. You are too good to me. It is what I have always wanted. Look. Look at how the finish is stained and worn, nearly gone in many places. Really, this is amazing. Look. It takes my breath away.

Colleen sat down on an easy chair. She looked at the rosary as though she had never seen it before, raised it to eye level, stared at the tiny crucifix dangling in front of her face.

—It's an antique, Wayne said. I bought it for you. It's a high boy.

CONSTELLATION

—A little used, Bill said, but what I'd give to hear the stories that furniture could tell.

—Bill can fix it up, Wayne said. Give it a complete restoration.

—Don't worry on that score, Bill said. When I'm finished, she'll be smooth as a shedevil's ass.

Colleen dropped the rosary onto her lap. —I'm sure. She shook her head. She sighed. —To know a lasting love was all I ever truly desired. It seemed little, when I was young, to ask of a world, this world, shot through with a multitude of possibilities. Remember when I was young, and was it really so long ago, so long ago as it seems now, although I remember it as though it were yesterday, things were very different. Who knew everything would change so fast, as I grew? We never expected America—America—the world, we never expected things to develop as they have now. When I was a girl, do you know what I expected? What I could expect? Well, I could be a nurse or a teacher or a wife. Or a dancer. That was the one standout, the one way in which one could assert herself. Oh, don't talk to me about movie stars. Yes, of course there were movie stars, but really, how can a movie star compare to anything? Really, Wayne, what does a movie star have to do with anything?

—How old do you think that desk is? Wayne said. Take a guess.

—I had a room, you know, Colleen said, the type of room a girl of my class could have been expected to have had during the period of my childhood. Oh, frilly things and dolls and stuffed animals—do I have to spell it out for you? You know what I'm talking about. And books. My family believed in reading, that reading was important, that somehow reading almost magically made someone a better person. It was, to them, an absolute value. So I was never short of books. From my earliest memories, there were always books around the house, in my room. I wonder sometimes what all those books were. It is impossible for me to remember them all. But inevitably some stand out, even now, across the gulf of vanished years.

—What if I told you, Wayne said, that high boy is over one hundred years old?

—Some of the books, Colleen said, were in a series. Books for girls, something like that. I suppose, really I know, there were books for boys as well. I wonder do such books still exist? I had a book, the title escapes me now, something about dance. *Dancers and Dreamers,* something like that. A big book with shiny cardboard covers depicting dancers in blue against a burnt yellow background. A cover like, I realized later, a badly imitated Degas. Each chapter covered a different dancer, her childhood, her struggle to perfect her form, her triumphant career. And after that nothing. No decline or death. The book, the chapter's rather, stopped at the dancers' peaks, the great victories, and moved on.

—Am I lying, Bill? Wayne said. This thing is so old, there isn't a nail, not one nail, in it.

—God's truth, Bill said. All wooden pegs.

—How long did I practice? Colleen said. Every day, day after day in front of my bureau mirror. Oh, I took lessons, early on, then my mother made me step out. She was frightened, concerned that I took it all too much to heart, and she made me stop. Later, as a teen, I took more lessons, but by then it was too late. I was too big, too heavy for the style of the day, and in my secret practice I had mistaught myself, developed a number of bad habits that proved

CONSTELLATION

impossible for me to fully correct.

The front door opened. Wolf came in with a woman on each of his arms. The women wore open fur jackets and thong bikinis and high-heeled shoes. One woman was a redhead; the other was a blonde. The blonde held a bottle of white rum.

—Hello, hello, hello, Wolf said.

—Hold my calls, Wolf said.

—Hello, Son, Colleen said.

—I want to talk to you, Wolf, Wayne said.

Wolf and the women walked to the stairs.

—You don't know what you want.

—I don't know what I want? Wayne said.

Wolf took the women upstairs.

—Where was I? Colleen said.

—Bad habits, Bill said.

—I don't know what I want? Wayne said.

—After the dance, I met him, Colleen said. We all knew each other in a way. We were a sort of loose group that socialized together, but until then I never really paid him any mind. He had a car, a Chevrolet, and that wasn't common in those days. We walked to the car and he wanted to drive out to the river. I knew what went on out there, we all did, and that night I thought, why not?

Colleen smiled. —Why not, I thought, just go?

—I know the feeling, Bill said.

Colleen nodded. —Yes.

—You get that feeling, Bill said, and you figure, why not?

—Yes, Colleen said. That's exactly correct.

—What the hell are you talking about? Wayne said.

—Of course, Colleen said, you don't want to think ahead. You feel like if you think ahead, if you

think one moment ahead, you'll kill something.
—Kill the moment, Bill said. That's a bad one.
—Bad, Wayne said.
—Bad or maybe not so bad, Colleen said, if you knew what was coming.
—What's coming is always a surprise, Bill said. That's what I like about life.
—What's coming is never a surprise, Wayne said.
Colleen laughed. —We thought, or I thought, no, I'm sure we all thought it would be Chevrolets and dances and rivers forever.
—Common enough mistake, Bill said. Hear it all the time.
—He was at his studies, Colleen said, and we installed ourselves in a three-room flat near the university. Afterwards, our first small house, the starter home. He had all the problems and promise of anyone in his situation—the horrible hours, the low pay, the brilliance, the big payoff out there ahead of us in the future.
—Wolf came along. Our new house, the burden of motherhood.
Colleen stopped talking, closed her eyes. Her head lolled to the side, rested on her right shoulder.
—I believe she's dropped off, Bill whispered. He nodded. —Tired out, the poor angel.
—His hours never got any better, but the money did, Colleen said. She straightened up and opened her eyes. Tears moved slowly down her cheeks. —Have to have been blind not to see, not to know, what I, hell, what everyone knew. I said nothing. I would not dignify him with a word. With a glance. He could have had the world from me, but he did not deserve shit.

CONSTELLATION

—Even the others weren't the worst of it, not the roaming, not the drinking. He still brought in money, so I could have put up with those things. And I had Wolf. They say now don't worry about the children, but Wolf, look at him, the angel, he's always been special to me.

—I heard this before. Wayne yawned. —I think it was on the radio.

—Him on all fours in the bathroom, Colleen said. Trembling. Shaking and vomiting while I held his hand. Try it sometime; it's a long way from the dance.

—Now which dance do you mean? Bill said.

Colleen stood up. —Yes. Back to work.

She went upstairs.

Two hours later, Wolf's women came downstairs.

—Where's Wolf? Wayne said.

—He fell asleep, the redhead said.

The blonde laughed. —He passed out.

—Exhausted, eh? Bill said. A day's work done well before quitting time.

—Quitting time for him, Red said.

Wayne went into the kitchen and came back with a six pack of tall boys. He pulled a can out of the holder and opened it. —Beer, anyone?

—All around, Bill said. Eh, gals?

—Sure.

—Why not?

—Did Wolf say anything about his mother? Wayne said.

Blonde laughed. —No. A lot of 'em do, though.

—That's not what I meant, Wayne said. I've got to talk to him.

He looked at Red. —What's your name?

—What's the matter? Red said.

—He gets nervous, Bill said. Drink up, Wayne. You'll feel fine. You girls work here, or are you traveling?

—Here for now, Blonde said. Sometimes we go someplace.

—Just floating along, Red said. She smiled at Wayne.

—The floating world, Bill laughed. —Well, it's all afloat, no goddamn doubt about it.

—What does that mean? Wayne said.

—What's the matter? Blonde said.

—Settle down, Honey, Red said.

Wayne finished his beer, crushed the can, set it next to his chair, and opened another. —I think you girls had better move along.

—We haven't finished our beer, Red said.

—Take it with you, Wayne said.

—Ah, let em finish, Bill said.

—Wolf said we could stay as long as we wanted, Blonde said.

—I think he wants us to move in, Red said.

The women laughed.

—Might not be all bad, Bill said. Have a few young women around the place. Lift some of the gloom, maybe.

—I said get out. Wayne pulled out his .44. —Go home, go home, go home.

—You better leave, Bill said. He's a little touchy this afternoon.

—Take the beer, Blonde said.

The women got up and went to the door.

CONSTELLATION

—Farewell my sweet swallows, Bill said. Fare thee well; your lives are hard, I know.

Bill stood up as the women went out the door.
—Drive carefully.

He waved.

Wayne and Wolf were eating microwave spaghetti at the kitchen table.

—If you have a dog, Wayne said, and that dog drags bad things into your house, what do you do?

—Sponge Boy's been roaming again? Wolf yawned. —A third of your life sleeping. Can't say I regret a minute of it.

A cordless phone rang on the counter.

Wolf stood up and grabbed it. —Yeah. No. Is there any proof? Okay.

Wolf hung up and punched in a number. —Bill, get over to the station and pick up the dog. Yeah. Better bring a cage and plenty of newspaper.

Wolf sat down. —How's Mom doing?

—I brought her some soup.

—You didn't bring home any of that meat, did you?

—What meat? Wayne said.

—From the dock. You find a box for the house?

—Hell no.

—Well, there was allegedly some spoilage. Little outbreak of something at some hamburger stand. Or chain, something like that.

—We're poisoning people?

—They can't lay this at our door, Wolf said. There's no way to trace that meat from the boxes.

—But it's ours?

—Could be anybody's. Anyway, some spoilage—that's after it left our hands. We're not responsible, the end user is. Naturally, you lose a little with anything. You know, the angel's share.

Bill came in the back door. —Your dog's in bad shape.

—That dog is supposed to be on a special diet, Wolf said. Who the hell has been throwing him meatballs?

Bill nodded. —Poison. Easy enough. Used to use anti-freeze, or was it brake fluid?

—I'm not sure, Wayne said.

—Someone's out to destroy us, Wolf said.

—I've got a vet on the way, Bill said. Am I authorized to put him down if it comes to that?

Wolf jumped up from the table. —Never. That dog can eat burning pitch. I won't have him destroyed because he's a little off his feed.

—First me, then Colleen, now this, Wayne said. Always comes in threes, doesn't it?

—We have to ask ourselves, Wolf said, who would want to ruin us financially?

—Didn't he just get some bad blood? Wayne said. Maybe lapped it up out there while nobody was watching?

—I told you, Wolf said. Don't lay this at our door.

—But if we're responsible, Wayne said.

Wolf slammed his plate to the floor. —Why can't people get it? In this country you're out for yourself, and fuck everybody else. Is that so hard? What's all this let's blame ourselves and plant flowers around the war memorial shit?

CONSTELLATION

Wayne ran to the living room windows. He was barefoot and wore blue pajamas. He looked out the window, ran upstairs, came down a few minutes later, dressed.

He shoved the .44 into his belt and covered it with his shirt. He jammed his bare feet into a pair of boots and went outside.

Bill stood at the hedge. Men with chainsaws were in the trees outside the yard. A bulldozer levelled a patch of earth.

—Power company? Wayne said.

—Naw, Bill said. He pointed to a pick up truck with a logo on its door. —Private outfit. Developers, I think.

Wayne watched the bulldozer. —That was all trees. They must have taken down a dozen.

Bill nodded. —Down in no time. You have to admire the equipment the boys have nowadays.

Limbs were falling from the standing trees.

—That's our land, Wayne said. They can't do this.

—Goddamn it, Wayne said. I planted some of those trees.

Bill looked at him. —You're getting carried away. Those trees were here before we were.

—That's not the point. Wayne reached under his shirt.

Bill caught his arm. —You better talk to Wolf.

—He did this?

—It's on the up and up, Bill said. Come back here with me and have a look.

Wayne followed Bill to the garage. Bill pointed to a cloth-covered box in the corner. Wayne shrugged. Bill pulled the cloth off the box: Sponge

Boy lay on his back, eyes closed, his four legs sticking stiffly up in the air.

—Dead. Wayne said.

—You'd believe it to look at him. Bill walked to the back of the garage and picked up a heavy piece of wood.

Wayne looked at the stick. It was part of a shovel or hoe handle.

Bill gave Wayne the stick. —Poke him and see if he'll move.

—You sure?

—Standard test, Bill said. The experts always use this one.

Wayne pushed the stick through the bars and gently prodded Sponge Boy's side. The dog did not respond. Wayne twisted his grip so he could brush the dog's side with the length of the wood.

He brushed the dog gently. —That's a good fellow. Good fellow you were, and now you're brought to a bad end with no memory of your service. No one knows or cares the good you've done.

Wayne inhaled deeply and wept silently.

—That's hardly a thorough exam, Bill said. Try your monitor on the head there; the brain may be the last to shut down.

Wayne flicked Sponge Boy's ear with the stick.

The dog did not react.

Wayne pushed back Sponge Boy's lips with the stick.

The dog turned its head, opened its jaws, caught the stick in its teeth. Wayne pulled back on the stick; Sponge Boy shook his head violently and wrenched the stick free of Wayne's hand. Wayne stepped back from the cage. Sponge Boy growled, shook his head, beating the stick against the bars.

CONSTELLATION

Bill laughed. —Lucky you didn't try that with your hand.

—If he could talk, Bill said, what do you think he'd tell us just now?

Sponge Boy kept beating the bars with the stick.

—Is he all right? Wayne said.

—Can't get upright, Bill said. The head's okay, but the rest won't move. I believe he was part paralyzed to start off.

—Will he get over it?

—He's better than he was. I'm leaving food outside the cage tonight, and he don't eat till he can walk out and get some.

Collen had her rosary strung around her neck. —Wayne, fix me a martini.

—I know I shouldn't, Colleen said, but I'll take a drop, for my heart.

—Listen, she said. The cicadas are back this year. Isn't it too soon? Time must be flying; surely, it seems too soon.

Wayne stirred the drink at the living room port-a-bar. —That's the fucking chainsaws.

—Your mouth is foul, Wayne. We have bodies, yes, and bodies have their uses, but must you be constantly vulgar?

—Oh, yes Ma'am.

—I will not dignify that comment. Colleen took the drink from Wayne, gulped it down, handed him the empty glass. —Another please, and put something in it. Eight to one; why can you not remember that?

Wayne set the glass on the bar and opened a beer. —Do it yourself.

Colleen walked behind the bar. —Rude, too.

She shook her head. —Not unlike my late husband. Useless, vulgar, rude.

—But really, Colleen opened the gin. —Really I should thank you.

She measured out the vermouth. —Always striving to keep me focussed on the reality of this world. Where is my dear son, Wolf?

—I don't know.

The back door slammed.

—Wayne, I got Chinese, Wolf shouted.

—In here, Dearest, Colleen said. Join us for a cocktail.

—Yeah, Wolf said. Wayne, give me a triple bourbon rocks.

—Colleen, Wayne said.

—Of course, dearest. I'll wait on you hand and foot.

Wolf flopped down on the couch and buried his face in his hands. —Jesus, what a day. Wayne, you see what Sponge Boy is like? Sure as hell wasn't bad meat that laid him out like that. Wolf paused, took out a handkerchief, wiped his face. —There's a neurotoxin at work here. If only he weren't so weak, I'd have him tested. Now I'm afraid he won't stand the loss of blood.

Colleen handed Wolf a glass of whiskey. He nodded and took a drink.

—Listen, Wayne said, is he gonna make it or not?

Wolf straightened up and put his handkerchief in his pocket. —You're right; business is business. I'll tell you this, though, as soon as I saw that dog, I knew

CONSTELLATION

he had fighting spirit.

 Wolf stood up. —I tell you this: If we had to stake everything on that dog, and we fucking well have, I'd take that bet in a heartbeat.

 Colleen shook her head. —This is inspiring. She set her glass down on the bar and clapped her hands. —My ears are ringing.

 —That's the other thing, Wayne said. What in the fuck is going on next door?

 —That? Wolf sat down. —They're putting up houses, I should think.

 —We're building rental property? Wayne said.

 —No, Wolf said. I sold off that land. We need cash, and those unimproved lots weren't bringing anything in. In fact, they were a loss. We were paying tax on that.

 —So there will be people living in our woods?

 —They aren't ours, Wolf said. And they aren't woods anymore.

 All the trees on the rest of the cul-de-sac were down. Wayne and Bill walked the graded earth beneath a crescent moon.

 —Look, Bill said. They've laid a few slabs already.

 —Kind of close together, aren't they?

 —I imagine they'll use fifty by a hundred foot lots, Bill said. Have room for ten, fifteen units in here.

 —Just what we moved here to get away from, Wayne said. Another fucking crowd.

 —There's only so much space, Bill said. And it's got to be filled.

 Wayne picked up a small branch and stripped

the leaves from it as they walked.

—Birddog was fifty years old, Bill said, and a solid two hundred. He still had the left hook from his days on the Harvard boxing squad. His father, one of the biggest ranchers in their western state, had sent him, his brothers, and, unusual for the time, his sister, east for the best educations that beef money could buy. Birddog knew even then, while he was studying oboe, that the greatest of the privileges his background had brought him was the land, the cattle and dogs and horses and guns and Indians—the experience of a land that was his crucible, his legacy, and he knew then, his destiny, which held him as surely as his skin held his flesh and bone and sinew.

—That's great, Wayne said. Terrific.

—Oh, Harvard brought him some things, Bill said. The knowledge of women, the company of books, the indoor, almost cloistered life expected of men of his class, men who would work, not among beasts from a beast's back on a broad plain beneath an open sky, but in offices, anchored to desks and controlling and controlled by briefs, reports, studies, channeling the river of language that channeled the nation and, in large measure, the world.

—When it was over, the four years on the quad with the too brief summers beneath the great thunderous and lightning-streaked skies of the ranch, Birddog took his leather-cased oboe and his framed diploma and the steamer trunk of his possessions and boarded a train that ran the century-old span from city to plain, east to west, pallid existence to the rough production of real value, of men and wealth that could be seen, touched, measured.

—And so Birddog crossed the continent, his future ahead of him like the towns and ranches strung

CONSTELLATION

out along the line, to find his father sitting on the front porch of the ranch house in the early evening with a glass of bonded bourbon in his hand and his favorite dog at his feet.

—Birddog looked at the old man, the black Stetson, broad denim-covered torso, the powerful hands that, on a bet, could bend a horseshoe nail into a bolo tie clasp, and the old man looked back at him and nodded.

—Here to claim your stake, the old man said, and he nodded again.

—Next day the old man put Birddog in charge of a thousand head at a far outlying camp, and Birddog's real education, his first true test as a man, began. Out there on the mesa with three ranch hands under him, Birddog weathered the long summer. He saw drought, fires, stampedes, flood, and his stock worried by bandits who made off with twenty head.

—That was nothing, less than they lost in a month to coyotes, but Birddog knew what he had to do. He brought his saddle and a .30-.30 to the bunkhouse at dawn and asked his men who was ready to ride. Two of the hands quit on the spot. The third, a boy of sixteen, grabbed his holster. Birddog shook his head. He told the cowards to get out and put the boy in charge of the herd. Then he mounted up and followed the bandits' trail. That was on the twelfth of July.

—Quite a story, Wayne said.

Bill sat down on the curb, took out a pouch of tobacco and papers, rolled a cigarette. He offered the pouch to Wayne.

Wayne shook his head. He threw the stick into a pile brush in the gutter. A jack rabbit flushed from the brush pile and ran across the pavement.

—The chase, Bill said, went on for months. He followed them over dry rock, up and down mesas, valleys, buttes, arroyos, always a little behind, a day late. Birddog grew hard in the saddle under that endless sky. The first snow found him in exurbia, a long way from Indian blankets and bridles and sheep-lined jackets, all the paraphernalia of a real life with the smells of coffee and bacon and hay and horses and straw and sweat and tobacco. The bandits had got the cattle in a truck. They may have had a copter as well—at the least, the signs showed they were dealing with somebody with a copter. Birddog swapped his horse for an old moped, wrapped his rifle in a bedroll on the back, sent his father a post card.

—He tracked them to a suburban packing plant, but by then those cows were beef, shipped south in reefer trucks, and the gang that stole them was long dispersed. Birddog doubted himself for the first time, but there was only one course open to him. He followed the meat. Followed it over the interstates to the Florida Keys where, in a bar beside a minimall, he met Boatcaptain, a Yale man with four tattoos and the washed out eyes of an ocean sailor of long standing.

—Now, Birddog had bribed the dispatcher, and he knew his meat was going, over-graded, to a supermarket in that minimall. Boatcaptain was a kindred spirit from his topsiders to the four inch scar on his left cheek. He had just dumped a load of drunken community college instructors who had fouled his boat and destroyed eight hundred dollars worth of tackle on a fruitless and hellish tarpon expedition, and he swore, between gulps of his strawberry margarita, that he was out of the tourism business for good. Birddog told his story, and the plan was hatched.

Wayne got up. Bill followed him.

CONSTELLATION

—Next morning at the loading dock, the truck driver found himself confronted by a man with a bandana over his face and a .30-.30 in his hand. The driver could tell from his eyes that the man was dead serious and wisely offered no resistance when the man's confederate locked him in a meat cooler and the two made off with the truck.

—Yeah, Wayne said. Terrific. He bent down and picked up some plastic strapping.

—Well, Bill said, they drove that truck, the whole thing now, right up onto the boat, and then it was over to New Orleans, up the Mississippi to the wide Missouri and—

—Yeah, Wayne said. He was trying to twist the plastic into a lariat. —Got it.

They were reaching the end of the leveled dirt.

—Did I tell you about how they hooked up with Maria and Juanita?

Wayne threw the plastic on the ground. —Another time.

—And Birdog and Boatcaptain sailed over the moon in a spoon, Bill said.

—That's a different story, Wayne said. Look at that.

A billboard had been set out by the curb. The legend read WELCOME TO BAKER'S DOZEN, and the board showed a fat man with rosy cheeks. He was wearing a white suit and chef's hat, and he was holding a tray of steaming loaves of bread.

Wayne shook his head. —Kind of out of date, isn't it?

—Ironic, Bill said. That is, or was, the style.

—Follow me, Wolf said. He carried a camp lantern out onto the dark lawn.
—Where? Wayne said.
Wolf shook his head.
Wayne followed to the garage. Wolf set the lantern on a plastic crate and took the cover off Sponge Boy's cage.
—Should I flip on the light? Wayne said.
—This lantern burns truer.
Wayne stared at the burning wick. —Huh?
Sponge Boy, paralyzed, growled.
—Nature and all. Wolf shook his head. —If I'd have geen thinking, I'd have looked to the future and put him to stud years ago.
—He's still growling, Wayne said. That's something.
—I can't see how this could happen, Wolf said.
Wayne sighed, paced around the garage. He went to the window, shielded his eyes with his hand, stared out at the dark lawn. Colleen, flashlight in hand, was walking toward the garage. She wore a flowing white gown.
—Boys?
—In here, Wolf said.
Colleen came inside. —Is he dead?
—The same, Wolf said.
—Bill was supposed to put him on a program, Colleen said.
—He's on a program, Wayne said. Number one for his demos.
—He looks the same, Colleen said. To me, he hasn't changed a bit.
—We'll have to go on, Wolf said. Rig something. We can't keep on like this; we're hemorraging.

CONSTELLATION

—It won't work, Wayne said.
—Surely, Colleen said, you could do something else. Something, for example, with dogs that sing.
—A whole show? Wolf said.
—Those singing dogs are hard to find, I think, Wayne said.
—Not dogs, idiot, Colleen said. Singers in dog costumes. A show where each character is a dog.
—Something people like, Wolf said. Something that speaks to the audience.
Wayne stood at the window. —Dark out there. Dog howling at the moon.

Twelve houses of BAKER'S DOZEN were sold. The thirteenth, the model home, went while the landscapers were putting down sod. Wayne watched the moving vans pull up, watched the lamps and recliners and dinette sets and couches and televisions and beds and chests and dressers and fitness machines unloaded, watched the families, all white and wholesome and unassumingly upper middle class, move into their houses.
At least the neighborhood had not gone to the dogs.
Everyone was settling in nicely: Even Sponge Boy was gaining some slight movement in his legs. Even Colleen was singing as she prepared meals or loaded the dishwasher in the evenings.
Wolf came in one night with a bottle of kirsch in one hand and a Chinese-made .45 in the other. He pulled the drapes in the front room. —How can they? How dare they?

—Who? Wayne said.

—We were up against the fucking wall when we sold that land. We started the fucking franchise. Our vision gave them everything. And now they come in legions to destroy us?

—What? Bill said.

Wolf waved the pistol. —Look around. We're encircled. The franchisees bought those houses.

—Shit, Wayne said.

—Goddamn, Bill said.

Wayne left the room.

Wolf handed Bill the bottle. The men drank in silence.

The back door slammed.

—Ma? Wolf said.

Silence.

—Where the hell is she? Wolf said.

Bill shrugged. He and Wolf walked through the house. They went out to the yard.

Wayne was standing beside the garage with a tarp laid out at his feet. His weapons, the .44, the .30-.30 lever action, a Bowie knife, lay on the tarp.

Wolf shook his head. —Your stuff's outdated. He raised the .45. —Even this, though I keep her for sentimental reasons.

—We're gonna have to fight these savages for our land, Wayne said. He pulled a bandana and a bottle of gun oil out of his pants pocket. —Better get yourselves ready.

Bill snorted. —For the range war?

Wayne, squatting by the tarp, was wiping down the rifle. —I'm ready.

—Why, I'll ride on the chuck wagon, Bill said.

—Yeah, Wolf said. We need to stake out the corral. Goddamn it, one little problem, any little

CONSTELLATION

stress, and he goes nuts again.
—Wayne grunted. —Nuts, am I?
—God, Bill said. Leave him here with his tarp.

Colleen stuck her head out the back door. Wayne was sitting on the tarp, feeding a small camp fire.
—Wayne, she called, time to eat.
Wayne stamped out the fire, picked up his rifle, rolled up the tarp, and carried his things into the kitchen. Bill and Wolf were at the table. Wayne leaned the tarp and rifle beside the stove, rinsed his face and hands at the sink, sat down.
Colleen filled a plate with food and set it in front of him. She served herself and joined the men.
Wayne picked up a piece of meat, gnawed on it, pulled a bone from his mouth and dropped it on his plate. —Tasty. Is it rabbit?
—Thank you, Colleen said.
—It's chicken cacciatore, Wolf said. You see the macaroni?
—Huh, Wayne said.
—We received an invitation in the mail, Honey, Colleen said.
—Huh, Wayne said.
—They want us to attend the Broadcasters' Ball.
—That's nice, Wayne said.
—I wouldn't be seen with those swine, Wolf said.
—You've been before, Colleen said. I never had the chance to go.
—I'm not much for dancing, Wayne said.

—I reckon all the neighbors will be there, Bill said. Dancing and putting on the feed bag.

Wayne forked noodles into his mouth. —This is really good.

—That's a thought, Wolf said. See all of them at once.

—Little something in the soup, eh Wolf? Bill said.

Wolf laughed. —What a terrible thought. Why that's like saying what if a car bomb were parked nearby.

—We never go anywhere, Colleen said. We never do anything.

—Plenty to do here around the place, Wayne said.

—We could go over and have a look, Bill said.

—We know who they are, Wolf said. What do we want to look at them for?

—Put a car out there and you'll get a lot of collateral damage, Bill said. And it's too dramatic. You'll have John fucking Law down your neck before you can say Jack Robinson.

—True, Wolf said. Besides, those idiots at the studio couldn't make what we need. I wanted a harness for the flying Sponge Boy skit; they couldn't make one. All of em took film and poetry when they should have been in shop.

Colleen looked out the window at the halogen lamp mounted on the peak of the garage. —Look outside, Honey. Everything's distorted. Even the glass distorts.

She picked up her goblet. —Wolf, open another bottle of wine.

—Easy, Ma, Wolf said.

—I'll do it. Bill got up.

CONSTELLATION

—We've got more to worry about than that, Wayne said. He pulled the Bowie knife out of his boot and stuck it in the table. —Time for vigilance.

—My table, Colleen said.

Bill filled her glass.

She looked at Wayne. —Right in my table! Now I suppose you'll have a little tale, a tiny anecdote, for your pals down at the bar room.

—Sorry, Wayne said.

—Sorrow, Colleen said. What on earth do you know of it? Could you know of it?

—Maybe, I, uh, Wayne said.

—Gone for days on end, Colleen said, and never a call. At first, I tried to resist. I'd shout and scream, throw things, cut up his shirts with scissors, throw his property out on the lawn. I would remind him of what he promised me, of the lasting love he swore was true, swore before me, before the community, before God. I scratched his face until the skin clotted beneath my nails.

—And it did not one bit of good. I should have known, should have seen, maybe did, maybe I knew all along, for all my histrionics, that I could not make him do as I wished. I could have killed him. That I knew. Very easily I could have taken one of his guns and shot him through the head or the heart. But I didn't want him dead; I wanted him back, back to the way he was at first, in the beginning.

—Never a word of apology or regret. Never even a word of anger or hatred or spite. That was the worst of it. He had been a garrulous man at the beginning, always ready with a story or a joke, particularly when he had a few drinks in him, but as he got older and things between us were worse, a silence grew up in him, grew, it seemed, from the inside out until I wondered, was he empty at the core?

—And if he was, how did he get that way? Everything came to him, came to him as though he were a magnet and things stuck to him like second nature. But it seemed I was cheated thrice: First when we planned things like trips to Paris but had not the resources to go, and later when cash was plentiful but he had no desire to go, and finally as you see today.

—I could have gone alone, but for what?

—Did I cause him to be the way he was? At the time, I knew it was all his fault, but now, in the distortion of memory, I'm not sure I know anything at all.

Bill got up from the table.

Wayne put his head down beside his plate.

—And then, Colleen said, he started up with those pills. Shaking. Vomiting.

She shook her head. —I'd find him passed out in the bathroom, on the front lawn, behind the wheel of his car. You try it. You start out one thing, and then you're holding him, mopping his forehead while he trembles and pukes as he kneels on the cold tile of the bathroom floor. That's the start of the whole long wasting and filth, the despair and sorrow and your inability to do anything at all. It's a long, slow way down, you'd never mistake it for anything else, that ends when they put what's left in a box and bury it in the dirt.

Colleen sighed. —Sometimes I wonder if anything is left.

She glanced at Wayne as though surprised his head was on the table, reached out, put her hand in his hair. —Asleep, Baby? That's right, you rest now. Rest.

CONSTELLATION

Wayne was throwing his Bowie knife at the garage. Sometimes it stuck and sometimes it didn't. He threw and retrieved, threw and retrieved, threw and retrieved.
Colleen watched from the kitchen. —Should we ask him again?
Wolf tugged at his cummerbund. —We've asked enough. Anyway, he'll be at it for hours.
—Well, Colleen said, as long as he's happy. She turned around. —Do I look all right?
—Stunning, Bill said. He adjusted his cufflink.
—Shall we take my truck?
—That wreck? Wolf threw Bill the keys to his Mercedes. —Take mine, but you're driving.
—Fine.
—You're designated, understand?
—Okay.
—I'm giving you the designation, driver.
—Righto. Bill turned to Colleen. —May I get your shawl?

At the hotel downtown, Bill surrendered the Mercedes to the parking valet and guided Colleen and Wolf through the revolving door and into a glass-walled elevator.
—How'd you know the floor? Colleen said.
—There was a sign, Bill said.
—Where?
—In the lobby, to the right of the door, between the elevator bays, Bill said. Where they always put them.
The elevator stopped. Bill led them to a

massive banquet hall. The tables were set up in the middle of the room, flanked by a stage and open area at the front and linen-covered bars around the back and sides. Uniformed waiters carried trays of *hors d'oevres* and wine.

—They're trying to fill us with discount chablis, Wolf said.

—It is cheaper, Colleen said.

Wolf frowned at his mother and said to Bill, —See if you can round up a liter of vodka. And no domestic or rusky shit, get the scandi.

Wolf and Colleen were seated at a table at the front of the hall when Bill came back with the vodka. A man in a tuxedo walked onto the stage and asked people to sit down. The banquet goers filed to tables, chatting, greeting, waving as they went. Several people approached Wolf to whisper greetings and shake hands.

—Look, Colleen said. They all know him.

Bill laughed. —Our little boy is growing up.

He raised his glass and he and Colleen toasted Wolf.

—We've got a special treat tonight, the man on stage said.

The lights went down and two spots hit the rear exits at either corner of the hall. A topless showgirl came through each door. One girl had a panther on a leash; the other had a tiger.

The crowd went wild. The girls and cats ascended the stage. The cats sat down, and the girls stood straight, flanking the podium.

—Let's get that food on the table, the master of

CONSTELLATION

ceremonies said, and get down to business.

Men in animal costumes carried platters of meat into the room at a run.

—The swine, Wolf said.

—Believe they're cows, Bill said.

—Sacred, do you think? Colleen said. She refilled their glasses.

—Why, Bill said, is everybody but us getting service?

—We have a special treat, the master of ceremonies said, and a bit of a surprise. Here, with a few comments for us this evening is the boy wonder of children's programming, Wolf Murphy.

Wolf stood up, bowed slightly, walked toward the stage.

The crowd was on its feet, the people chanting—DOG, DOG, DOG.

Wolf went up the steps, nodded to the showgirls, shook hands with the MC. The MC left the stage. Wolf raised his hands to quiet the crowd.

—Thank you, thank you, thank you. You'll be happy to know that I have not prepared, and I will not give, a full speech to distract you from this superb repast.

They started up again —DOG, DOG, DOG.

Wolf raised his hands. —I am happy to report that Sponge Boy is well on his way to recovery. At this very moment, he is resting comfortably under the watchful eyes of my uncle Wayne.

The crowd broke into applause.

Wolf nodded. —Thank you. Now to my scattered and brief remarks.

He nodded again. —That we provide a vital service is, must be, and henceforth ever will be a given. No more need to discuss this old saw than the air

which envelops us. Particularly the news divisions have defined their roles as reporters, interpreters, and creators of the vital questions of the day.
—But what of us in the entertainment end of the media? Are we mere clowns? Or perhaps an extraneous, a superfluous appendage, a function of an intersection of history and technology, a meaningless frill riding parasitically on the real society and economy?
—Or perhaps we function to reflect and humanize the deeper concerns, oppositions, and contradictions of the culture at large.
—Both assumptions are fundamentally false: Entertainment is neither frivolity nor culture, but commerce. Commerce and communication. What began as a delivery system for product advertising has evolved into product itself while retaining its initial function.
—Now what have we to look forward to? I think we all know—more entertainment. Technology's here already, awaiting the hook up, to give us nigh infinite choice. This is no small thing. You know the numbers—not just domestic revenues, but as an export factor, we're selling more entertainment than cars. Figure entertainment into the trade deficit and you know what happens.
The crowd laughed. Some chanted —JAP, JAP, JAP.
Wolf nodded, smiling. —So what do we have? A valuable commodity in communication itself? True, but much more than that. We have the fruit of leisure, entertainment. Industry has led to the industry of the future. And the demand for entertainment continues to increase. All of human history, agriculture, industrialism, the difficult, grim,

and oft-times bloody road of mankind's progress leads here, to the demand for and eventual delivery of more entertainment.

The crowd applauded wildly.

Wolf bowed and walked to his seat.

Bill wiped his eyes with a linen napkin. —I was moved by the power of your language.

There were toasts and greetings and plates heaped with meat and condiments.

Wolf stumbled a little on his way out to the car.

—Those phony bastards, Colleen said. Smiles and shakes.

—Shit, Wolf said.

—We should have served them poison for drink, Bill said. The fucks.

—I could have taken the lot of em with a .22 rifle, Wolf said. Some threat. Some enemies.

Maybe he had shut his eyes, dozed off for a second, though Wolf had only leaned his head back and intended to rest, but yes, he remembered looking at the dark buildings and the halogen lights and then, for a moment, it seemed everything was dark and the car had gone round and round a telephone pole, hit the pole, bounced off, bounced back into the pole, and wrapped itself around the pole. Wolf could feel the warm blood run down his forehead. He mopped it up with his handkerchief.

Bill had been driving with Colleen beside him; Wolf was in the back.

He mopped his forehead again. —Goddamn. Everybody all right up there?

—Fine. Colleen's voice was weak. —I'm sure everything is fine.

—Huh, Bill said. Hah. Ugh. Yeah. Ah, that's it. All right. Righto.

—Goddamn, Wolf said. Saw the whole thing, but I saw it from an ariel view, outside, above the car. Like I was out of my body watching it all.

Colleen struggled with her door. —We better get out of here.

Wolf and Bill tried the other doors, then Colleen's. They could not open any of them. Sirens sounded in the distance.

Colleen sighed. —Wait, wait, wait.

—I hope she doesn't blow, Wolf said.

—Well, Bill said, call me bullethead. Don't know how she got away from me. Seems like I had my foot on the brake for the semaphore and the foot started cramping like I was holding her in the wrong position and I got to thinking about would I let go. Worst thing, that damn thinking. Then she just went.

—You had a fit, Baby, Colleen said.

Bill sighed. —A love fit, perhaps.

Men with special equipment cut them free from the wreck.

At the hospital, a nurse put a butterfly bandage on Wolf's forehead. Doctors shown lights in their eyes and told them they were okay, lucky, lucky to be okay. After the quick examinations, they were released.

Wayne was asleep in his bedroll beside the garage.

They saw no reason to wake him.

CONSTELLATION

Wolf took the day off. At noon, he was in his robe, drinking coffee and looking through the paper.
Bill came in. —He's at it again. Had the rifle aimed at the neighbor's house. Then he turned it on me. Said he didn't know who to blast.
—He's playing, Wolf said. Hell, he's just a big kid at heart.
—I'm staying away from him.
—Yeah, let him alone until he comes to his senses.

Wolf walked up behind Wayne.
Wayne threw his knife at the garage. —You don't make any noise, do you? You know any rope tricks?
—I'm not going to restrain you, Wolf said. He took a tin of little cigars from his pocket and lit one up. —So, you're all fucked up again?
Wayne turned around. He pointed to Wolf's forehead. —They let a bit of blood out of you, boy.
Wolf spat out a shread of tobacco. —That's nothing.
He spat again. —Come in the house and knock this shit off.
Wayne shook his head. —Enemies in, enemies out. I'll stand this ground.
—Those neighbors will be out in our own time. Don't give em a free show.
Wayne walked to the garage, pulled his knife from the wall, walked back to Wolf. —I will be Commander of the World.

Wolf snorted. —An Eskimo would be dead at your age.

Wayne squinted and slowly nodded.

—Anyway, there's no one against you in the house, Wolf said. Come in; you can play with your radios.

Wayne thumbed the knife blade. —Am I the King of the Living who in splendor knowingly awaits his horrible doom?

—Get off it, would you? You know you're talking to me here.

Wayne pointed to the kitchen window.

Bill was watching them.

—I'm not going to let some fucking dead guy rule my house, Wayne said. He waved the knife for emphasis. —Not now, not ever.

—You were there, Wolf said. You carried Bob to his grave.

—I never put my hand on that casket.

—Not literally, Wolf said. It would have been inappropriate for a member of the immediate family to bear pall. Anyway, and this is the part of my job I like least, quit the crazy shit or I'll have you locked down and shocked up .

Wayne held the flat of the knife in front of his face. —I am surrounded by threats to my health. He glanced at the .30-.30 on the tarp.

Wolf tossed the cigar butt on the lawn. —What is it you want?

Wayne's arm went limp. He dropped the knife. —I'm bad off. Fucked up. Crazy in the head. The worst is it happened in here.

Wayne tapped his temple. —All on the inside. Did it to myself. Or my chemicals did it to me.

He picked up the knife and threw it as hard as

CONSTELLATION

he could at the garage. It penetrated to the hilt the thin upper panel of the single door.

A dull low whine came from inside the garage.

—What the fuck is that? Wolf said.

Wayne stiffened, his eyes wide. —Dead Bob.

—Sponge Boy! Wolf said. Christ, have you been feeding him?

—That's Bill's job.

—He's afraid to come out here, you fucking maniac. How could I trust you? How could I forget? Wolf ran to the garage.

Wayne followed.

Sponge Boy, on his back, whined.

—Get me a bowl of milk and the turkey baster, Wolf said. He rolled up his sleeves.

Wayne ran to the house.

—Easy, boy, Wolf said. Those bastards. Crazy and whining—they never had a real problem in their lives.

He put his fingers through the bars and stroked Sponge Boy's head. —You're worth a hundred of them.

Wolf shook his head. —Sick, and those idiots left you to die. Why don't they just drive a stake through my heart?

Wolf folded his arms on top of the cage, began to weep, leaned forward, his head on his arms. —It's all me, me, me with these candy asses, while some of us work for a living.

Wolf sobbed, rolled on the garage floor, foamed at the mouth.

—Give him air, Colleen screamed. Clear off.

GREG MULCAHY

Wolf opened his eyes. —Air.

Colleen, Bill and Wayne stood around him. Wayne was holding a steel bowl with a turkey baster in it.

Bill squatted beside Wolf and eased him up into a sitting position. —Okay, now? No numbness? See blue halos? Can you talk all right?

Wolf coughed, cleared his throat, turned his head and spat on the garage floor. He looked at Sponge Boy. —Did anybody think to give him air? Take him out and put him in his place in the sun?

—I'll take him out, Wayne said.

Wolf got up and took the bowl from Wayne. He filled the baster, squatted, syringed a little milk into Sponge Boy's open mouth. After a second, the dog bit down on the plastic barrel.

—He won't take much, Wolf said. Can't. Perhaps he's sick of it all. I hope, if it goes bad, he'll die tired. That may be the only mercy.

—Shit, I lived tired, Colleen said. What do you know about it?

—All right now, Bill said, the lad's ill.

—It's the dog, Wayne said. That dog is sick.

Wayne stayed in the house nights and put his weapons in his room. He wore the pistol, but he kept it covered. Bill fed Sponge Boy every day, and Wayne rigged the cage on some wheels and curtain rods so he could take the dog out into the sun. Sponge Boy regained his weight and looked his old self, but there was no change in the paralysis.

Every morning, Wayne pulled the cage around the neighborhood. He was at the end of the development, at the street that formed the entrance to the cul-de-sac, when he noticed the sign, a big, yellow, plastic banner strung between the street lights. Red letters spelled out:

CUL-DE-SAC FESTIVAL
BAR-BE-CUE
GAMES
FUN FOR ALL

and the dates. Dates for the last weekend of the month.

Wayne hurried home, pulling the cage quickly behind him.

Wolf and Bill were examining something on the front lawn.

—Look at that, Wolf said.

Bill shook his head.

Wayne looked. There was a dead cat, a tabby, on the lawn.

Wayne scratched his head. —It's dead. Probably went on a treated lawn. Poisoned. Maybe ate a poisoned rat; I think that happens—the poison gets right into the cat, and that's it for him, poor fellow.

—Poor fellow? Bill said. Don't waste your tears, boy. His troubles are done. Bill laughed. —Done for now at least, though maybe he has eight sets left.

—Laugh and laugh, girls, Wolf said. You ignorant bitches.

—The dog is better, Wayne said. Much better. Have a look. Then lay off the insults.

Wayne let go the cage handle and straightened up. —There's a limit, Wolf, even for you.

—That's not the point, Wolf snapped. He

pointed at the cat. —You know what this means? This is a little message from our neighbors. What was out here yesterday, Bill?

—Bit of trash. Cups from a fast food place, sandwich wrappers. I figured some kids tossed them out a car window.

Wolf smiled. —And now a dead cat? Ever here of escalation? He walked to the elm tree on the boulevard. —Look at this.

A green poster advertising the cul-de-sac festival was stapled to the tree.

—That's what I came to tell you, Wayne said. They got a banner over the street.

—So it's a neighborhood now, Bill said. We should have thought about that going in.

—Should have is history, Wolf said. What do we do about it now?

—What I wouldn't give, Bill said, for a couple spools of detonating cord.

—Yeah, Wayne said. But where to get some? He yawned. —Anyway, I've got a sick dog to worry about.

—Backing out now? Wolf said. Hell, you were right before. They want to bury us.

—What happened to my wife? Wayne said. Colleen? I meant to have her call the exterminator. We're infested, aren't we?

Next day, three bags of garbage on the lawn. No one had heard anything during the night. Bill cleaned up the mess while Wolf dressed. He came out in a dark suit, white shirt, scarlet tie. Wolf carried a leather briefcase. He got in his car and tore off down the street.

CONSTELLATION

He returned several hours later.

Wayne was in the room full of radios. He had taken out Sponge Boy earlier; now his time was his own. The radios were on, tuned, he thought, to one station, but the feed was cluttered and staticky. Wayne heard an announcer saying, *Mother, you had that problem with Dad.* He could not be certain. Maybe the voice was saying, *Those Romanians changed everything.* Or maybe it was something else altogether.

Wolf was calling him.

Wayne switched off the radios and went downstairs. Colleen, Bill, and Wolf were drinking ouzo in the living room. Wayne got a beer and sat down on an easy chair.

—It's like those tigers that dance on the ball in the circus, Wolf said. We're on the ball, but it moves in spite of our claws. We've got to stay on top.

—What does that mean? Colleen said.

—Indeed, Wolf said.

—Seems clear enough to me, Bill said.

—All that money you thought was yours was lost a long time ago, Wolf said. The lawyers filed the bankruptcy papers this morning.

—A black abyss with a whirlpool, Wayne said. The maelstrom awaits us now.

Bill filled his glass. —It's a subterfuge. He lifted the glass to Wolf. —Shrewd business. What next? Move the station to Mexico and call Sponge Boy Spongito?

Wolf groaned and looked at Wayne. —I'm not that far from where you're at. I get down more than you realize. When I think of what we've got in relation to what there is to have—shit, we got nothing. High-tech, aerospace, weapons—not the fucking guns we sold, real weapons systems—securities, pharmaceuticals—fuck, we didn't have a taste, we didn't have a fucking crumb.

—We all feel bad sometimes, Colleen said. I could mope around all day, left with regret and wishes, dreams of what I should have done with the now dead.

Wolf stared evenly at her. —You don't understand fear yet, Mother. But you will. He took a swallow of his drink. —I fear for myself, certainly. What else? And if I cared for anything else in this world, I'd fear more deeply for that thing.

Wayne noticed the strap of a shoulder holster under Wolf's jacket. He looked ar Wolf's feet. There, above the right shoe, was the tell-tale bulge of an ankle holster.

—Maybe we could do a cowboy show, Wayne said.

—Story of? Bill said. Episode of?

—Shut up, Bob, Wayne said.

—Bill, Bill said.

—The devil and the devil met the devil on the road, Wayne said.

—Wolf doesn't need this, Colleen said.

Wayne walked into the kitchen. Colleen, Wolf, and Bill were eating turkey sausage and frozen waffles at the table.

—Glad you're here, Wayne said. All together now—

—Sit down and eat, Baby, Colleen said. She pushed out a chair. —You'll need your strength.

—Too busy, Wayne said. He held up a heavy, black-bound book. —I'm going to cure Sponge Boy with this.

CONSTELLATION

—That? Bill said.

Wayne scowled at him. —This book belonged to Bob.

—Good luck, Wolf said. He jammed a chunk of waffle into his mouth. —The doctor or the dog.

Wayne was gone for six days.

He came back with the book and a bottle of rum. The book was in tatters, the pages loose from the binding, soiled, creased, held inside the worn covers with rubber bands. The rum bottle was half empty.

—Everything will be all right, Wayne shouted.

No one answered. He went into the living room.

—Isn't it wonderful, he shouted. Isn't it wonderful.

Wayne went to the staircase. —It's fine.

No answer.

—Isn't it wonderful. Wayne heard the back door open. —The recovery has begun.

Colleen ran in and hugged Wayne. —At last, she said.

—I am the King of Fire, Wayne said.

—I've been all alone, Colleen said. For days now. Bill out roving, Wolf at the station, and you, you I didn't know where.

Colleen stepped back. —You smell like a dog.

Wayne nodded. —Wonderful. He kept nodding.

—I think we'd better get you a shower and into bed, Colleen said.

—All right. Wonderful.

Wolf was singing. Wayne opened his eyes, and that's what he heard, Wolf singing:

First we'll have some whiskey,
Then we'll have some gin,
Then I'll take you in the back room,
And teach you how to sin.

loudly and off key.
    Wayne jumped out of bed and ran downstairs. Bill was smoking a cigar in the living room.
    —Where's Wolf? Wayne said.
    —Too late, Bill said. He wants to remain undisturbed for awhile. Bill switched on the tv with the remote. —We've got some tennis coming on.
    Wayne sat down. The tennis matches seemed endless. Wayne could not understand the scoring. He asked Bill about it, but the explanation did not make any sense to him. Bill ordered a pizza. They ate. The matches kept going on. Bill crouched on the edge of his chair, watching intently. Wayne looked at the ceiling. He counted the little holes and dabs of texture in the paint.
    Red and Blonde came down the stairs.
    —You, Wayne said.
    Bill stood up and bowed slightly. —Charmed ladies, how charming of you to favor us with your presence.
    The women laughed.
    —Aren't you going to offer us a seat? Red asked.
    —How about a beer? Blonde said.
    Bill waved them into the room. —Of course. I forget myself. Wayne, there's a half case cooling in the fridge. Could you be an angel and get it?

CONSTELLATION

Wayne groaned, stood up, went to the kitchen.
—Some day, Bill said, we really must have a chat about your work.
—Our work? Blonde said. What the hell do you do all day?
—This and that, Bill said.
Wayne came in with the beer and handed it around.
—Bit of a Jack of all trades, Bill said. He winked.
—And you want to know about ours, Red said. You want a real complete description?
—Oh, yeah, Bill said.
—What about you? Blonde said. You like to listen?
Wayne shook his head. —Not for me.
The women laughed.
—Loosen up, Baby, Red said.
—Not for him, Blonde said and laughed.
—There's something for everybody, Bill said.
—You would not believe it, Red said.
—Such sweet little swallows, Bill said. Innocent, yet you know more than most.
—There's that word again, Blonde said.
—Word? Wayne said.
—Swallow, Red said. I put out my arms and the swallows came and landed on them. They stayed there, cooing gently.
—Swallows that coo? Bill said.
—We called her Lady of the Swallows, Blonde said.
—Shove off, Bill said. I saw that movie.
Red said, —You did?
—I wish we could, Blonde said. Wolf keeps making us act it out.

Wayne found Wolf in Bob's old den.
Wolf sat writing at the desk. He scribbled, raised the paper before his eyes, read, —Having gained the world—
—Wolf?
—I didn't hear you come in. Wolf took off his half glasses. —Just catching up on some work.
—I didn't know you needed glasses.
—For reading, mostly. Purely magnification. Though sometimes they're good for the image. You know, business meetings.
Wayne laughed. —You don't have to tell me.
Wolf nodded, unstoppered a cut glass decanter, poured out two drinks. —You seem happy, Wayne.
—That bother you? Wayne took his drink.
—No. It's refreshing.
—You'll be happy too, Wolf. Wayne raised his glass. —I cured him.
Wolf stood up and backed away from the desk. —By him, you mean yourself? You mean Wayne's all better now?
—No, Wayne said. Sponge Boy.
—You cured Sponge Boy?
—Well, half cured. He can move one side, the right side of his body.
—The right?
—Maybe it's the left. Hard to tell. You know, point of view.
—Yes, Wolf said.
—I predict a complete recovery, Wayne said. In time. Obviously, these things take time. A time to

CONSTELLATION

heal, and so forth. But when he's on track, our worries are over.

Wolf sat on the edge of the desk. —Yes and no, Wayne. He pushed a button on the intercom. —Bill, could you get in here, please?

Bill came in. He was carrying a can of beer and his shirt was hanging out of his pants. —Yeah, what now?

—He claims he cured Sponge Boy, Wolf said.

—Shit, Bill said.

—Well, half cured, Wayne said.

—Sponge Boy's an asset, Wolf said. He's insured. We've already depreciated him.

—Now you can appreciate him, Wayne said. He filled his glass. —We win both ways. Wayne turned to Bill. —Gave him a lot of things. Mostly vitamin E. Nature's miracle.

—Go get the cattle prod, Wolf said.

—Why not shoot him? Bill said. Got a silenced piece in my kit.

—We want the status quo for now, Wolf said. Who knows, Wayne might be on to something.

—Oh, Wayne said. I'm on to something. He reached to his waist; the .44 wasn't there. He was wearing pajamas.

—We need to take our time and think, Wolf said.

—Just so, Wayne said. I'll get dressed.

—Stay there, Bill said.

—Quiet, Wolf said. First we need to look at the poor beast. He's in the garage?

—Yeah, Wayne said.

Wayne dressed quickly, checked the cylinder of the .44, jammed his knife into his boot. He heard them come back into the house and went downstairs.

Wolf was holding a ball peen hammer.
—Okay, you got what you wanted.
—Give us what we want, Bill said.
—What? Wayne said.
—Where the fuck is the dog? Wolf said.
—I told you he's in the garage.
—Gone, cage and all, Bill said.
—He was out there.
—Big man, Bill said. Take off that gun, Johnny, and I'll teach you who's a man.
—Don't put this on me, Wayne said.
—Where's the fucking dog? Wolf said. He sat down on the couch. —I don't need this. He dropped the hammer and cradled his head in his hands. —This I don't need. Not now.
—Tough guy, Bill said. He jerked his head toward Wolf. —Look what you're doing to him. He gave you everything, and this is how you repay his kindness.
—I didn't take the dog, Wayne said. When I came in last night, he was in his cage in the garage. Answer me this: Was the door open when you got there?
—Who pays attention? Wolf said.
—Yes, Bill said.
—Yes, what? Wayne said.
—Yes it was open. Wide open. Wide fucking open for all to see.
—Yeah? Wayne said. I locked it last night. I left the light on too, to keep Sponge Boy company.
—It was off, Bill said, or burned out.
—Let's have a look at the bulb and lock, Wolf said.

CONSTELLATION

The light bulb was intact. The lock plate was scratched slightly, but Wayne could not tell whether that was from normal wear or from an attempt to pick the lock.
    —Why turn off the light? Wolf said.
    —To operate in darkness, Bill said.
    —Out of habit, Wayne said.
    —Why take the dog? Wolf said. Why not just kill it?
    —Somebody knows what it's worth, Wayne said.
    —He's on tv, Bill said, everybody knows what he's worth.
    —They want to humiliate us, Wolf said.
    They looked for footprints, tire tracks, foreign objects, physical evidence. There was nothing.
    —It's not like we call the police, Wolf said. We wait. Maybe they'll demand ransom.

    Wolf sent Wayne to check out the studio. Nobody was there. The kids who operated the station had fled or been laid off. The sets were covered with dust. Wayne's circus wagon was listing in a corner, one of its front wheels gone.
    No trace of Sponge Boy.
    All the cameras, cables, mikes—everything was gone. Wayne's office was empty. In Wolf's, he found some old newspaper, pornographic magazines, and a half bottle of mescal.

At dinner, Wolf forced them to give their reports.

—Nothing at the station, Wayne said.

Bill had been through the neighborhood. —Complete appearance of normality except for a portable stage a truck hauled in. For the festival, I guess.

Wayne and Wolf looked at each other.

—They would not dare, Wayne said.

—They'll do anything, Wolf said. You'll see.

—You pulled out on them, they sued, Bill said, you got a restraining order, they bought out Baker's Dozen—

—What fucking difference does the goddamned story make? Wolf said. They're against us, that's all.

—Those fuckers never would let us breathe, Wayne said. Even now, they keep taking my picture.

—Huh? Wolf said.

—Out there. Wayne pointed to a tree in the darkness outside the window. —Look, in the crotch.

—Video camera, Wolf screamed. He pulled his .45 out of his jacket and fired seven shots through the window.

—I trimmed that today, Bill said. There's no camera.

—What happened to Ma? Wolf said the next night. Her car's gone.

Wayne was staring out the broken dining room window. —They say ghosts walk on the waters at night.

—Haven't seen her now for three, four days,

CONSTELLATION

Wolf said. When's the last time you saw her?

—It doesn't worry me, Wayne said. How could it? I must have been out of my head.

—Great, Wolf said. Could we address the subject at hand?

Wayne stared through the broken pane. —I had a vision once, a beautiful vision of the most beautiful thing, and I tried to get it out of my head, but I could not.

Wolf sang, —Gain and loss is the law of life / I believe I'll take a drink tonight.

—Now I look out into the gloom and I see the desolate strand and the bodies, the dead of Ireland and Italy, Europe and Africa and Asia covering the waves while the coffin ships in the distance, at that far horizon, disgorge more and more.

—That's history, Wolf said. Don't read all that shit if it upsets you. Now where the hell is Ma?

—Past, present, and future I see, Wayne said.

Wolf shook his head. —This asshole's mad again.

He went into the living room.

—The living and the dead, Wayne said. All together. What mystery. The living will be dead, but the dead will never live again. That is the difference.

Bill found Wayne on the dining room floor the next day. He yelled for Wolf. Wolf came in from the den. He was wearing a telephone headset. Bill pointed to Wayne's prostrate form.

—Tele-meetings all day, Wolf said. Rouse him or leave him.

Bill went out to the garage and got a heavy,

long-handled shovel. He ran the blade over Wayne's face. —Look alive, boy. We'll have no more slacking here.

Wayne opened his eyes and tried lazily to push the shovel away.

Bill jabbed him with the point. —Don't handle the merchandise.

Wayne smiled. —Here to bury me?

Bill gripped the shovel like a baseball bat. —Might clout you, boyo.

Wayne sat up. —A spade. There's the peasant's weapon. He lifted the pistol from his belt and held it loosely, barrel pointed at the ceiling. —Ever here of this?

Bill raised the shovel. —Let go the gun, you crazy fuck.

Wayne stuck the pistol in his belt. —Crazy? I got tired and I went to sleep. Isn't that what they say? You're supposed to eat when you're hungry and sleep when you're tired. Doesn't everyone agree on this?

—Just the thing, Bill said. He lowered the shovel.

—Who are you to question me in my own house? Wayne said. He stood up, stretched, rolled his neck. —Bit of stiffness. That's where you fall down. All I've been through, everything always against me, and what then? Then some little fucking thing, anthropod, bad cell, microbes out there to lay you low. They never quit. Programmed by nature to always continue.

—Yeah, yeah, Bill said. Let's light some candles, and we'll all have a good cry.

He had the butt of the shovel on the floor, and he ran his thumb over the blade. —Take a taste of the file.

CONSTELLATION

—When I was a boy, Wayne said, we'd go to these lake cabins in the summer. Rickety old shacks, more or less, but it was summer, so what more did you need?
—That's the most fascinating remembrance, Bill said. He pounded the shovel on the floor. —I guess that child remains within each of us, huh?
—Resorts, we used to call them, Wayne said. Seems kind of comical now, the word *resorts* for these little ramshackle shacks on the edge of a lake.
—Language. Bill shook his head. —It's what seperates us from the animals.
—Of course, bits and pieces of it are stuck in my mind, Wayne said. But what really struck me was the turtle shells. Giant shells, maybe two feet in diameter, nailed to the trees.
—With the turtles inside?
—No, these were empty. And I had to wonder, why should they crucify these snapping turtles?
—Like the bones, Bill said.
—I guess, Wayne said.
—No, Bill said. Those bones nailed to the wall of the garage out there.
Wolf stood in the doorway. —I did that.
—Raccoon? Bill said. Got the night bandit in our garbage?
—One of the neighbor's dogs, Wolf said. Give them something to think about.

The half moon was high over the cul-de-sac. Three or four figures in dark clothes were far down the street, like stick figures, talking perhaps, too far away to be heard. They moved around something, their arms swinging in the air, the glint of metal in the moonlight. The echo of a hammer far off. Leaves fell in the light breeze, landed gently on the lawns, sidewalks, streets. Leaves mounded in the gutters, yellow, orange, red, raked into long low rows, the colors bleeding, losing their values in the darkness.

Something moved, a dull rustle in the leaves, cat or squirrel or rat. The crisp, cool air. Clouds moved over the moon above the half-naked tree limbs. That echo, the hammering, a low frame, sticks placed by stick men, a quadrilateral arrangement, the outline of a box taking shape in the darkness, with the echo, echo, echo of the hammers, the swings, short arcs ending in contact, of the stick men in their dark garb down the street.

No birds. Too late, perhaps, for any birds. The birds now at their roosts, too late for anything, perhaps, except an owl. No owls here. A dog barked and a truck, a pick up, ran rough and slow on a side street, a branch artery, a hub off the main line, the slow truck going somewhere, roughly, but not loud, not too loud, and the dog barking, barking at the truck perhaps, or at the men, or at the leaves in the soft wind, or at the echo of the hammers.

Lights in the windows up and down the street, lights behind the mini-blinds and drapes visible sometimes as fields, squares through the blinds or lines between the drapes, closure inexact, imperfect, unresolved. The light obscured, imprecise in the crisp air, bright windows in contrast to the dark windows, the silent entryways, closed doors, empty cars in the driveways, parked in darkness as though abandoned in the dark driveways beside the silent houses, half-lit, unevenly lit, lit and dark, dark and lit, up the street and down the hub streets, similar, familiar, identical.

CONSTELLATION

Something in the air, something he had smelled before, but not easy to immediately identify. Not the normal smell, the once normal fall smell of burning leaves; no one burned leaves anymore. It was, perhaps, illegal now to burn them. But something was burning. Wood. Wood from the wood-burning stoves, the fireplaces. The smell of wood fires and motor oil and raw pine.

Wayne walked to the garage, out of the stickmen's line of sight. He saw the bones nailed beneath the apex of the roof, glowing, or if not glowing, absorbing the moon-and-star light, more bright than the normal gray/tan/off-white of bones.

Wayne nodded. —You too. He nodded again.
—If I were your age, I'd be dead by now.
Wayne nodded.
—Not that they'd have me on display out here.
Wayne nodded.
—Have me hidden away, they would. Better still if I just disappeared.
Wayne nodded.
—Have me disappear, that would be the best thing. Go out, go out on an ice flow and be left there with my memories. Left alone with inside of my head.

Pounding on the door.
—Open it, goddamn it, Wolf said.
—All right. Wayne got out of bed. —Just a second. He put his robe on over his clothes, went to the door, unlocked it. —What?
—When did she go? Wolf shouted. I need the day. The time.
—She's been gone, Wayne said. He cinched

the robe belt. —You know, I thought she was just out.

Wayne put his arm around Wolf and steered him down the hall toward the staircase. —I know you're upset. As am I. At first I thought, oh, well, she's just out. Then I thought, well, perhaps she went for a visit. See her relatives, you know, or a sick friend. Time went by. No call, no letter. Needless to say, I never found a note.

They descended the staircase.

—You didn't, did you? I thought not.

Wolf shook free of Wayne. —But when?

—A while back. I know she's your mother. I know it hurts. Wayne spread open his arms. —But I'm hurt, too. No one, believe me, no one hurt me more than she did.

Wayne walked to the kitchen. Bill was reading the paper at the table.

—When? Wolf said. We've got to get this pinned down.

Wayne shook his head. —It won't help.

He sat down at the table. —We have to go on. First, a hearty breakfast. Hey Bill, how about whipping us up some kippers and eggs? I've always wanted to try that.

Bill leaned back, his chair on two legs. —You didn't tell him? He sighed, leaned forward, put his face close to Wayne's. —All the radios are open. She took the backs off them.

—Maybe some English muffins, Wayne said. Have we laid in any of those?

—Money, Wolf said. She got out of here with money. And who knows what else—gold, gems, negotiable bonds.

—Dead Bob's hidden treasure, Bill said. I never thought there was such a thing.

CONSTELLATION

—She swore there wasn't, Wolf said.
—No matter, Wayne said. It's hard, but I wish her well. Sincerely. Anyway, how about those eggs?

Wolf had the headset on, but the cord had been cut about six inches below the earpiece, and it dangled near his shoulder. —The lawyers say there's nothing we can do. No insurance coverage, nothing but paper left of the station. Worse, they want to be paid. Some shit about a lien on the house.
He pulled the .45 from his shoulder holster and paced the living room floor. —They're getting us bit by bit, like we're the piglet and they're the snake.
Wayne looked at the ceiling. —What have we got in reserve?
—Reserve? Wolf laughed, stopped laughing, snapped, —Where the fuck is Bill?
—I don't know.
—That slippery bastard. Let him leave the ship. We'll go it alone. That's how we started, Wayne. We'll get Sponge Boy back and start again without a fucking thank fucking you very fucking much. Where's your rifle?
—Upstairs.
—Keep her oiled up.
—I suppose.
—You too? What do you want now?
—I think, Wayne said, I think, what I want is to go back to my car. My Comet. Seems like I left it someplace. Forgot about it for awhile. But it's out there somewhere. Maybe could use a little work, to get her up and running, and then—
—That's not coming back, you stupid

motherfucker. You're the kind of guy who's driving a hundred, and when some idiot jumps in front of the car, yells DON'T.

A car door slammed.

Wolf ran to the window. —There he is. He holstered the .45. —Don't mention what I said; I lost it there for a second.

Bill carried in a sealed cardboard carton. —Little help, boys. There's more in the car.

They carried in box after box:: noodles, cheese, beans, flour, oil, tomato paste, canned vegetables.

—Where'd this come from? Wayne said.

—Old pal at the warehouse store. We're stocked for as long as it takes.

—How we fixed for booze? Wolf said.

—Check the basement, Bill said. Believe your lovely mother left us ten or twelve cases.

—Ammunition? Wayne said.

Wolf uncrated three Chinese MAK 90's. —Sporters. What the fuck did Dad want with these?

—Same action, Bill said. He passed a rifle to Wayne. —Grab a rag and try to get the fucking cosmoline out of this.

—Yeah, Wolf said. They're jammed.

—Practically sticks to my hand, Wayne said.

Wayne rubbed the rifle with part of an old flannel shirt. He opened the action and jammed the rag into it. —I'll stay with my Winchester. She's tried and true.

—We could use a Dragunov, Wolf said. Sit up in the attic window and take em one by one.

—Long distance is the next best thing to being there, Bill said. Why not go all out, wish for rockets?

CONSTELLATION

  —We don't have access, Wolf said. He had his rifle disassembled and was scrubbing the bolt with a kerosene-soaked toothbrush. —You know, sometimes I find myself wishing I knew more about technology and less about finance.
  —Especially the latest bitter lessons, Wayne said.
  Bill shrugged. —You take a risk, you might win, you might lose. Thing is to dust yourself off and keep going.
  Wayne ran a cleaning rod down the barrel of his rifle. —Where are we going?
  —Neutron bomb, Wolf said. I can't imagine that would be so difficult.

  —Hold on, Wolf shouted. Goddamn it, hold him down, Wayne.
  Wayne grabbed the handcuffs by the chain and pushed down with all his strength, forcing Bill back onto a kitchen chair.
  Wolf poured hydrogen pyroxide into the gash on Bill's face.
  Bill struggled, screamed—Jesus Christ—tried to get up, tried to rock the chair back.
  Wayne held tight. —Easy, easy.
  Wolf pressed gauze pads onto the wound, taped them to the skin. He stepped back. —That better be all he's got, cause that's all we're treating.
  Bill sat limp, his head hanging, eyes closed.
  —Did you cuff him? Wayne said.
  Wolf shook his head. —He said last night he was going to get a magazine and have a swallow. This morning I found him on the front lawn like this.

—Who did it to you, Bill? Wayne said.

—Bill, Wolf said, can you hear me?

Bill raised his head and opened his eyes. —Who are you people and why are you torturing me?

—C'mon Bill, Wayne said. Maybe we should cut those cuffs off him.

—I got a key in the bedroom, Wolf said. But let's wait till he comes to his senses.

—Give him a drink?

—Couldn't hurt, Wolf said.

Wayne filled a small snifter with brandy and held it to Bill's lips. —Down the hatch.

Bill drank, coughed. —Not bad. Not the best either.

—He's coming around, Wolf said.

—Come around to what? Bill said.

—You know, Wayne said. Just relax.

—Who are you?

—Well, who the fuck are you? Wolf said.

—I, uh, I—I don't know, Bill said. He shook his head. —Funny, it's slipped my mind. Got any more of that brandy?

Wayne gave him another drink. —At least you can identify brandy. That's the first step.

—Yeah, Bill said. It's funny, I can't seem to remember a goddamn thing.

—Hit him again, Wolf said.

—Don't even know my own name, Bill said.

—How could that happen? Wolf said.

—I was struck by lightning.

—Bullshit, Wolf said.

—I was run over by a train.

—I know how it happened, Wayne said.

—Bill, you've got to come back, Wolf said. The festival's in two days.

CONSTELLATION

—Festival?
—Fisherman Bill, Wayne said. More like Bob Blank.
—We'll put him on something, Wolf said.
—What? Wayne said.
—I don't know. Special diet. Exercise videos.

Bill, wrapped in a Navajo blanket, sat in front of the fire Wolf had made. He was calm; the handcuffs had been removed several hours earlier.
—Here's what I remember, Bill said. At the river, the path is steep and clayey, but there are pebbles in some parts, in the low washes, I guess they are, but mostly clay, rutted and packed hard, sometimes with a little grass, trampled to be sure, pushing through, the path as it winds around and down the banks, steeply, winds steeply, and you can hear the water running, the green water, and smell something green and moist and maybe a little rotten, and flies and gnats and mosquitos swarm around your face and keep swarming.
—What use is this to us? Wolf said.
—Could be the start, Wayne said. Maybe he'll get it all back.
—Or, Bill said, early in the morning, in the winter when the weak sun comes up a dull yellow disc behind the clouds and the sky is banded a soft pink and a flat light gray and you know the snow is coming, later in the day that snow will be coming down in one of the infinite varieties of snowfalls, one flake or a few or many and large or small and heavy or light.
—Do you think, Bill, Wolf said, that you could drive a car?

—Or garden? Wayne said. You remember how you always loved working out in the yard?
   —Or, Bill said, on a dark night, dark as it gets without clouds, with no clouds and as small a moon as the moon gets small when you're far from the city and all the light and noise and reflection and you come through the trees to a clearing and look up, and see the bright arrangements of the stars and recall the stories of this place, the tales of violence and hatred and metamorphosis that named the constellations we dwell beneath.
   —What? Wayne said.
   Wolf pointed to his head. —Esta muy loco.
   —No me jolas, Bill said.
   —Wayne, we need beer and snacks. Come help me in the kitchen, Wolf said.
   In the kichen, Wayne said, —What?
   —He's fucking dead weight for us now. Unless we can get him to drive.
   —That's no job for anybody.
   —He won't know the difference. Hell, just keep listening to him. Talk to him if you have to. We've got to win back his trust.

   Wayne put more wood on the fire. The coffee table was covered with beer cans, ashtrays, dip containers, snack bags. Wolf had stumbled upstairs a few hours earlier. Bill, wrapped in the blanket, sat, eyes open, his head drooping to his chest.
   Wayne opened a beer and sat down on the couch. —Have another, Bill? Okay. Anyway, sometimes I wake up alone in that bed and think that I can not live without her. It feels like I can't take

CONSTELLATION

another breath. Do you think she'll come back, maybe not right away, but after awhile, you know? Sometimes you blank guys know things, don't you?

Wayne yawned. —I remember when Bob and me were boys. Fighting each other with bricks, hammers, pipes, baseball bats. We really went at it. And Dad, good old Dad, drunk as a drunken sailor, sailing in drunk and giving us the money from his pockets like a drunken sailor on a drunken spree.

Wayne wept. —And now, to hear them talk as though these were bad things.

Wayne grabbed another beer, knocking several empties off the table. —Is this what life is made of? This is the texture of life?

—What'd you get? Wolf said. He was sitting at the foot of Wayne's bed. —Can he do this thing for us?

Wayne lifted his head. —She's gone, Baby, she ain't coming back. He dropped his head to the pillow.

—These guys are just the start, Wolf said. After them, we move down the line. Politicians, doctors, lawyers, journalists, teachers. Get rid of all of them and prepare for the new order. Are you with me, Wayne?

—Shut off the loud speakers. Wayne put his forearm over his eyes.

Wolf wore a long white apron. —Let them have their little bar-be-cue; we'll feast this afternoon on lasagna.

—Where's Bill? Wayne said.

—He's out in the car practicing. I've got him backing in and out of the driveway.

—How's it going?

—He has a little trouble with reverse, but I don't think that will be much of a problem.

—Have we got some semplex?

—Naw, Wolf said. We just have to do our best with what's at hand.

—Harder to trace anyway, Wayne said.

—If the driver gets caught, they'll have nothing out of him.

The telephone rang.

Wolf picked it up. —Yes.

Wayne opened the oven door.

—Yes.

He looked inside. The oblong pan was covered with foil. The foil was smooth and neatly creased around the edges of the pan.

—Yes.

Wayne gently closed the oven.

—What can one say? Yes.

Wayne took a glass from the cupboard and filled it with red wine.

—I understand. Monday morning at ten. Yes. Wolf hung up. —They're sending a sheriff's man round for the house and contents.

—We'll be gone by then, Wayne said.

—Funny, Wolf said, the sheriff's man. I knew we had a sheriff, but I never thought they still sent officers out on seizures.

Wayne shrugged. —How else?

—I know. I just never thought about it.

The phone rang. Wolf picked it up. —Who? Yeah. Okay. I understand. No, no. We don't want

CONSTELLATION

that. Yeah, sure. Okay. Fine. Thanks.
 He hung up.
 —Sheriff again?
 —Nope. That was the head of the cul-de-sac committee inviting us to the festival.
 —Just like that?
 —Bygones be bygones.
 Wayne shook his head.
 —Yeah, Wolf said. I'm sure they'd like to have us there for the main event.
 A band began to play, far off. The national anthem.
 —Hadn't we better start on our project? Wayne said.
 Wolf took off the apron and draped it over a chair.
 In the garage, Wolf pulled a large plastic tarp off some blue fifty-five gallon drums. —Here it is.
 The drums had the word INFLAMMABLE stencilled on them in bright yellow paint.
 —What are we using? Wayne said.
 —Not sure. We had this stuff at the station, and we couldn't get rid of it. Damn garbage men wouldn't haul it off. Wolf walked to the driveway. —Bill, bring the car.
 Bill backed the Roadmaster to the garage, shut it off, got out. —I'm doing fine. It's all coming back to me—shift, gas, brake.
 —Great, Wolf said. He popped the trunk.
 —Carburetor, alternator, spark plugs, battery, water pump, heater core, fan, fan belt, valve, lifter, head gasket, starter, Bill said.
 Wayne jammed a drum in the trunk. —I don't think another will fit. Can we get two in the back seat?

—Bit of a squeeze, Wolf said. He rolled a drum to the rear passenger side door. —But we'll make her.

—Tie rod, axel, manifold, muffler, tail pipe, bushings, transmission, master cylinder, Bill said.

—What are we gonna use for a trigger? Wayne said.

He and Wolf wedged a drum sideways between the front and back seats.

—That's the problem, Wolf said. Our letter of credit fell through before the Swiss or the Czechs or whoever they are could ship it. I hate it, but we'll have to rely on collision.

—Tried and true, Wayne said.

Music started up again.

—Listen, Wayne said. It's an accordian.

—Uh uh, Wolf said. Bells. Chimes, I think.

—I'd know it anywhere, Bill said. The call of the gypsy's guitar.

—Go inside, Wolf said. Take a nap. Wayne and I will finish this.

After the spoon-full-of-water relay, the sack, three-legged, and piggy-back races, the softball game, darkness fell on the festival. The air was rich with the smells of burning wood and charcoal and roasting chicken, suckling pig, beef. The platform became a stage fully equipped with lights, sound system, and banners proclaiming the greatness of the land and of the festival itself.

Inside the house, Wayne heard a garbled voice through a bull horn. He ran to the kitchen. —Are they calling us out?

Bill sat at the table.

CONSTELLATION

Wolf was slicing tomatoes at the counter.
—It's the PA system. They're organizing something.

A band struck up a march. Wayne and Wolf went to the living room and looked out the window.

—Goddamn, Wayne said.

The families and organizers of the festival formed up in long ranks behind a high school marching band. The adults held torches they had lit from a huge bonfire behind the platform.

The band started down the street. The drum major held what appeared to be a giant luau lantern. The crowd, three or four abreast, followed the musicians.

—Bill, Wolf said, wait for us in the car.

Wolf and Wayne returned to the kitchen.

—Sit, Wolf said. He put a pan of lasagna on the table and sliced it into squares with a chef's knife.

—What about Bill? Wayne said.

—He'll stay in the car. Wolf poured some wine. —I told him he could eat when he got back. Wolf served them each a square of lasagna. —We'll eat a little, let the parade go by, then send him on his way.

Wayne nodded, his mouth full of lasagna. The marchers were passing the house.

—I forgot the salad, Wolf said. He got up, took two bowls out of the refrigerator, set one in front of Wayne, sat down and began to eat from the other. —Bill's out there watching them through the windshield. Big thrill for him. Goddamn shame he had to turn out this way.

Wayne nodded and took another piece of lasagna. —You never know.

—That's for sure, Wolf said.

—Never know one fucking day from the next. Then you look back and you have to think, why was I

149

so blind? What was wrong with me?

Wolf poured Wayne more wine. —Well, now.

Wayne ate some salad. He chewed, looked at Wolf, set his forearms heavily on the table as though he were exhausted, as though he did not know what the fork in his left hand was for.

—I had everything and a car besides, Wayne said. And still it seemed like there was something wrong with me.

The marching band trailed off.

—They'll be finished soon, Wolf said. Don't get yourself all wound up now.

—When this is over, Wayne said, what I'm thinking is, I'll put an ad in the classified section. Something she can see out there to show how much I want her back, so even if she doesn't come back at least she'll know.

Wolf wiped his mouth with a checked cloth napkin. —Listen.

Somebody was saying something through the PA system.

—They're back. You about ready?

Wayne nodded.

Wolf threw threw the napkin on the table.

—All right, Wolf said. You're all ready for this? He ran his hand over Bill's shoulder belt. —You're sure you know what you have to do?

Bill nodded.

Wolf massaged Bill's neck and shoulders. —Head straight for the platform. Don't let anything stop you. If the car flies into the bonfire, don't be afraid. Just get out and run.

—Okay, Bill said. Got you.

CONSTELLATION

—Drive carefully, Wolf said. He slammed the driver's door shut.

No one made anything of the car. Bill pulled out and turned slowly toward the festival as he had been instructed to do. The street was not closed; the barricades that had blocked it during the parade were awaiting city pick up on the curbs.
Wayne and Wolf sat by the picture window. The lights in the house were off. They watched the Buick crawl up the street toward the platform.
—Shouldn't he be speeding up? Wayne said. You told him to go fast, didn't you?
Wolf lifted a pair of binoculars to his eyes.
—He's slowing down. Shit. He looks like he doesn't know where he is.
—You can see his face?
Wolf waved the binoculars at Wayne.
—Combloc night vision. Not as good as ours, but cheaper.
—He's stopping, Wayne said. I'm feeling funny; maybe it's time to bury the guns and fade away.
—Maybe it's time, Wolf said, for you to move into a building that looks like a file cabinet, you simple fuck.
—Okay, genius, look at the car.
Bill had pulled the Roadmaster neatly into a space between a GMC truck and a Japanese sedan.
—What's he looking at? Wolf looked through the binoculars. —There's nothing to look at except the guy on the platform.
Wayne was breathing hard. —What is the matter?
—Car maybe. Could be mechanical failure. All

this, and my fucking car can't go a block. Where's Bill? Did he get out? You see him get out? Is he on the floor?
—Did he pass out? Wayne said. Was it too much for him?
Wolf ran into the den and came back with an elegant double-barrelled shotgun. He looked through the binoculars. —Leak? Is that a pool under the car?
Wayne went out the front door, pulled his revolver, pointed it at the car.
Wolf pushed Wayne out of the way, broke open the shotgun, jammed shells into the chambers. —These are special. Incendiary. Hope to hell I've got the range.
—Never saw that gun around, Wayne said. She's a beaut.
—It's Dad's old Hemingway. He kept it hidden. Wolf raised the gun, aimed at the car, fired.
The car went up in a ball of flame.
—FIRE, Wayne screamed.
—WATER, Wolf yelled. Shit.
Water spewed like a geyser from beneath the car.
Sirens sounded in the distance.
—The city's on fire, Wayne said.
—Burst the water main, Wolf said. Why couldn't the gas main go?
He pulled Wayne into the house. Wayne slipped and fell on the living room floor.
Wolf grabbed Wayne's pistol and shoved it in his belt. —Wouldn't want to fall on this. I'll hold it.
He went into the den and came back with a gasoline can in each hand.
Wayne tried to stand up; he could not control his feet. A fire truck was outside. Red light flashed on the walls.

CONSTELLATION

Wolf poured gas on the floor, the couch, the chairs. —This is a problem. He worked his way into the dining room.
Wayne crawled to the staircase. He grasped the banister, tried to pull himself up.
—That truck will be gone in no time, Wolf called from the kitchen.
Wayne thought he saw fire everywhere. Or water. Spraying water with fire light reflected everywhere in the droplets. He heard the firemen shouting outside.
—First, Wayne said, my heart was broken, and now apparently my legs as well.
Wolf had his coat on. He held the shotgun in one hand and a stuffed leather briefcase in the other.
—Can't move, huh? He shook his head. —I hate to leave you like this, Uncle, but it's time to go.
—Poison me, you fucks? Wayne said.
—You're the only thing I've got that's redeemable for a cash value. Wolf sobbed. He set down the case and wiped his eyes with the back of his hand. —Sorry. My fault. Anyway, it'll be quick. A spark from the pilot, whatever. Why, there might even be some type of remote in my truck. I'll have to check. This is terribly unfortunate, but we lost our place on the highway to the future.
Wayne crawled up the first step. —I've got the antidote. Got me a box full of antidotes if I can but limp or crawl to it.
Wolf lifted the case and straightened up.
—One really must go on. All this talk—this language—what is it but air?